dirty words

dirty words

provocative erotica by m. christian

 alyson books
los angeles | new york

MANUFACTURED IN THE UNITED STATES OF AMERICA.

THIS TRADE PAPERBACK ORIGINAL IS PUBLISHED BY ALYSON PUBLICATIONS,
P.O. BOX 4371, LOS ANGELES, CALIFORNIA 90078-4371.
DISTRIBUTION IN THE UNITED KINGDOM BY TURNAROUND PUBLISHER SERVICES,
UNIT 3, OLYMPIA TRADING ESTATE, COBURG ROAD, WOOD GREEN,
LONDON N22 6TZ ENGLAND.

FIRST EDITION: FEBRUARY 2001

01 02 03 04 05 **a** 10 9 8 7 6 5 4 3 2 1

ISBN 1-55583-563-5

LIBRARY OF CONGRESS CATALOGING-IN-PUBLICATION DATA
  CHRISTIAN, M.
    DIRTY WORDS : PROVOCATIVE EROTICA / BY M. CHRISTIAN.
    ISBN 1-55583-563-5
    1. EROTIC STORIES, AMERICAN. 2. GAY MEN—FICTION. I. TITLE.
  PS3553.H7274 D5 2001
    813'.54—DC21   00-045402

CREDITS

• "Dirty Deeds for Dirty Boys (And Men)" © 2000 by Patrick Califia-Rice. "Blue Boy" © 2000 by M. Christian, first appeared in *Embraces: Dark Erotica*, edited by Paula Guran. Venus or Vixen Press, 2000. "Casey, the Bat" © 2000 by M. Christian, first appeared in *Men for All Seasons*, edited by Jesse Grant. Alyson Books, 2000. "Echoes" © 1997 by M. Christian, first appeared in *Grave Passions*, edited by William Mann, 1997. "How Coyote Stole the Sun" © 1997 by M. Christian, first appeared in *Happily Ever After*, edited by Michael Thomas Ford, Masquerade Books, 1996. "Matches" © 1997 by M. Christian, first appeared in *Grave Passions*, edited by William Mann, 1997. "Spike" © 2000 by M. Christian, first appeared in *Best Gay Erotica 2000*, edited by Richard Labonté. Cleis Books, 2000. "The Harley" © 2000 by M. Christian, first appeared in *Butchboys*, edited by Michael Thomas Ford, Masquerade Books, 1997. "Wet" © 1996 by M. Christian, first appeared in *Sons of Darkness*, edited by Thomas S. Roche and Michael Rowe. Cleis Books, 1996. "What Ails You" © 1996 by M. Christian, first appeared in *Southern Comfort*, edited By David Laurents, Masquerade Books, 1996.
• Cover photography and design by Philip Pirolo.

To all those wonderfully, fantastically, deliciously dirty words.

Contents

Acknowledgments

While writers often work in isolation, we are never really alone: The people who have encouraged us, held our hands, or just left us alone while the words demanded our attention are always with us. For me, the following are just a few of those precious people:

To my dear friends who are also writers (and so understand): Patrick Califia-Rice, Thomas S. Roche, Starlight, Simon Sheppard, Bill Brent and Puma, Michael Thomas Ford, Carol Queen and Robert, and Dick Freeman.

To my dear friends who are also editors (and so who not only understand, but also appreciate): Susie Bright, Amelia Copeland, Cecilia Tan, Maxim Jakubowski, Richard Labonté and Laura Antoniou.

To my dear friends who are also publishers (and so who are all of the above): Scott Brassart, Angela Brown, and all the other great folks at Alyson Books.

And to my very dear friend who isn't an editor, publisher, or writer (and so who has no excuse): Martha.

Foreword

Dirty Deeds for Dirty Boys (and Men)
By Patrick Califia-Rice

It can be very damned awkward to have a good friend who is also a writer (or who wants to be one). What do you do when someone approaches you for an introduction or a blurb for the back cover...and you like their wicked smile or their spicy chicken marsala or their hospitable, fuzzy butt a whole lot more than you like their paragraphs, which are as graceful as a football tumbling down the stairs, and filled with mixed metaphors and fuck scenes that could not be resurrected with a truckload of Viagra? Fortunately for me, M. Christian presents no such dilemma. Given our long and intimate acquaintance, I probably can't be 100% objective about the book you are holding in your hot little hands. But I can honestly say that this is some of the best writing, period, that I've perused in the last year.

Be forewarned: *Dirty Words* is not a walk in the park on a sunny day. Like many quiet and unassuming people, M. Christian conceals a frightening intellect, a lurid imagination, and a Zen comprehension of the evil that men can do. In case you never have the privilege of meeting him or hearing him read, I'd like you to know that he's a really nice guy. Honest. Sweet. Compassionate. But all of those virtues spring from doctoral-level study of the Shadow. His kindness is informed by a sad appraisal of all the self-interested alternatives. He chooses not to exploit others even though he gets exactly how thrilling it can be to push a weaker person down and suck them dry.

The best writing about sex is also about something else. The San Francisco writers I refer to as the Glamorous Nerd Pornographers are handcrafting a renaissance of smart smut. Like *Fanny Hill, My Secret Life,* or *Dangerous Liaisons* (bet you didn't know that was originally a very banned book), sexually explicit work by Carol Queen, Thomas Roche, M. Christian, Bill Brent, Ian Philips, Kirk Read, and their fellow travelers creates a record of mores, manners, philosophy, fashion, controversy, politics, religion, and other keynotes that preserve the tenor of a given moment in human history. (As do a handful of great sex writers in other locales, like Tristan Taormino in, uh, what is that place? New York City?)

The themes that preoccupy M. Christian include (but are not restricted to) revenge (in "Chickenhawk" and "Counting" he details the way a pursuit of vengeance alters the agents of Nemesis as well as her object), the signifiers of masculinity (two badder-than-bad bikers in "The Harley" compete for possession of a dead bro's hawg), the odd things that can cause one human being to bond with another ("What Ails You"), and the Crisco-slippery, razor-sharp twists that Fate loves to hand out to those who think they already know how their story is going to end

("Matches"). Oh, and cock sucking. I don't think I've ever encountered a writer who is more poetically obsessed with cock sucking than M. Christian. He is a bard of deep throat, a lyrical celebrator of the profoundly transformative act of blowing a load all over somebody else's tonsils. He's a dab hand at describing ass fucking as well. But there's a difference between the three-star restaurant and the one that gets four stars. M. Christian has paid his dues, watching the habits of the feral, big dick (his own and others) as assiduously as your maiden aunt noted various species of swallows in her bird-watching log, or monitored the ownership of cars parked after dark in other people's driveways.

There's a lot of pretty violent stuff in this book (see "Blue Boy" for a prime example). But even the most horrific acts become as jubilant and aesthetically pleasing as a machine-gun massacre in a Quentin Tarantino film. And there's always a surprise. M. Christian does not take the easy way out. From the relentless way he works his readers' nerves, one might almost suspect him of a certain amount of sadism. He's also a surprisingly moral author—never preachy, but never slipping into the sort of gratuitous bloodshed that quickly becomes a big yawn. There's no noir character more overworked than the vampire, but M. Christian puts a new spin on it with a melancholy artist who feels obligated to clean up the mistakes he makes when his loneliness becomes too much to bear ("Wet").

The carefully choreographed pseudoviolence that's called sadomasochism in the postindustrial West also figures heavily in these stories ("Spike" and "Puppy"). But these are not the hackneyed stories that make one fall asleep over most of the remaindered paperback product of Masquerade Books. "Spike" is a tour de force about narcissism that would make the most seasoned psychiatrist seek out his own psychoanalysis, and "Puppy" pokes good horny fun at every stereotype of the autocratic and omniscient Master.

It will no doubt become apparent to you before you've flipped very many of these pages, pumped the bottle of Sex Grease a few times, and dug out a clean (or at least cleaner) come rag, that M. Christian is a talented writer of horror as well as science fiction, mythology, and porn. This synthesis of horrorerotica reaches a peak, in this book, in "Echoes." I'm not sure I wanted to know this much about necrophilia, but now that I do, it is probably building my character even as I type this introduction.

But my favorite stories in *Dirty Words* feature that irrepressible trickster god who is probably the patron saint of queers. I am talking about Coyote himself, blood brother of Loki, Set, and Elegba. In "Coyote and the Less-Than-Perfect Cougar" and "How Coyote Stole the Sun," M. Christian perfectly captures the cringing and fawning facade of this master thief and Back Door Man. Coyote has his priorities straight. He's not afraid to flatter the pants off you as long as he gets those drawers down around your ankles.

You can shoot Coyote. You can poison him. You can trap him and hang him and throw him off the cliff or lock him up in jail, blow him up, starve him, and flatten him with a steamroller. But he'll always pull himself together and be back tomorrow night or in a fortnight, making good use of the intelligence he gathered during his fatal foray at your defenses. Sooner or later he will walk off with your cherry, your cash, your car keys, your boyfriend's virtue, and your most cherished illusions. When you've been (literally) fucked over by Coyote, you emerge a sadder but wiser person, and not really all that sore, considering you've just been banged by the sacred phallus of the Father of Lies.

Coyote represents the persistence and survival of the downtrodden, the not-particularly-deserving poor. He is able to take joy in life even when the conditions around him are unbelievably bleak. He is ingenious, creative, fun-loving, and apparently irresistible. Coyote knows what's behind propriety (and chances are, has been in that behind). He knows who is unfaithful, who sleeps with the stone of a guilty conscience in his bed, who harbors "unnatural" desires. To Coyote, this is all grist for the mill. Because he is free of the normal prohibitions that regulate right-thinking mortals and gods, he always keeps his mobility. The most severe punishment cannot turn Coyote aside from his pursuit of carnal pleasure, comfort, and advantage over others. He teaches us to respect the aspects of ourselves that we would much rather disown. Because when we pretend to be obedient and righteous, all that repression and self-delusion distracts us from the here and now. We leave the chicken coop unlocked, and Coyote gets a free meal. Or we forget to satisfy our loved ones' dirtiest impulses, and Coyote gets a quick and shabby but ecstatic fuck on your clean sheets.

That brings us back to where we started, with some highfalutin talk about the Shadow. Jungian psychologists believe that when we are most cut off from these disavowed and dangerous emotions and actions we become depressed, impotent, and unable to do any real good. We may be frightened or disgusted by the faces of the bastard children of our own spirits, but they are often the most energetic, vivid, and real parts of ourselves. Pornography exists to keep the Shadow of a monotheistic and ransacked world alive. As long as one person can write about or film ribald acts that flaunt the status quo, and somebody else can read or watch this heresy and beat off hard enough to take off like a helicopter, magic will be kept alive, and along with it, our best hope of salvation. (Which we achieve, paradoxically enough, only when we abandon the gloss of being pure or holy.)

Pornographers are thus the fitting heirs of the trickster archetype. It's no surprise that this genre of entertainment is banned as often for its political satire, attacks on the church, or lampooning of other sacred cows as it is for being too plainspoken about the Old In and Out. In *Dirty Words*, M. Christian has a prolonged romp at the expense of homophobia, several flavors of People of the Book, butch iconography, pacifism, pulling out before you come, selfishness, prudery, bullying, virginity, and monogamy. Put your ear closer to this page and you will hear an outraged mooing. Then go get your reading glasses and your poppers or whatever accessories you require to luxuriate in a good dirty book, and savor, relish, enjoy, get it up and get it off, and laugh yourself sick and sane.

Under the name Pat Califia, Patrick Califia-Rice has edited and authored many collections of sharp-edged and discomfiting erotica and is one of the founding members of the modern, so-called leather community. (Ha!) He lives in San Francisco with partner Matt Rice and their son, two cats, and two stepdogs. He also has a private practice as a therapist. In his spare time, he quilts, gardens, makes grand pagan schmattes, and does ornamental body carvings.

Preface

Of all the things I've written, this has got to be the toughest.

Want a story about an ancient Native American trickster God looking for "stuff?" Sex beyond death? A world of disposable people? Dick-dueling bikers? A lonely immortal who has to make a terrible choice? No problem.

But write about myself? Now that's a problem.

It's not like I haven't written about myself before, or that I'm a shy recluse. I'm actually out there quite a bit, if you know where to look, but that's the public self, the on-the-street self. It's not the deep, dark, perverted me.

You see, telling stories about things like piercing, bondage, fisting, and other twisted things is damned delightful. Want a story about a dwarf who preys on chickenhawks? Bittersweet stories of loss and redemption? Rampaging stories of butt fucking and hydraulic blow jobs? How many words do you want and when do you want it?

But that's just telling stories, and telling stories is fun. But it's hard to write about me, about writing, because writing is my kink, my fetish, and a powerful one at that.

It's hard to write about a kink when it's my own.

But I can tell you that I love to write. Noir, humor, nonfiction, horror, fantasy, science fiction, poetry, plays, smut—you name it. Yeah, I have to do the McJob thing to eat, but my fingers itch and ache to get back to working on the story of the moment. Even though I don't always write about sex, for me, writing is very much a sexual thing. Hell, it even kinda follows the Sexual Response Cycle: Excitement (an idea comes to mind), Plateau (putting it together), Orgasm (riding the high), and Resolution ("The End").

So you could say you're holding multiple orgasms right now.

I hope you like these stories, and that they make you smile, shiver, cry, laugh, and get wet and/or hard.

Because it was good for me too.

— M. Christian

Spike

Matching, same, identical—Spike and Spike were fooling around behind the barn.

No, that's a lie—but merely a location slip. They were definitely fooling around—Spike sucking on Spike's cock while Spike fondled his brother's quills of starched blond hair—but they weren't cocksucking, getting cocksucked behind the barn. Urban equivalent: Spike opened his throat and took eight inches of his brother's pale dick meat until it danced with his very well-trained gag reflex in an abandoned mattress factory in the Mission District. Just the two of them and the skittering dance steps of invisible rats in the walls—urban equivalent of mice, cows, and horses.

The mattress factory was their favorite fuck spot. Yeah, rats. Yeah, plaster dust like a liquid itch on whatever rubbed against it. Yeah, it smelled—fuck, no—it fucking *reeked* of crackhead piss, butane, and wine. But it was their place, and it was close enough to Bebe's so they could suck and fuck themselves into a quaking-kneed palsy then stumble over to sack out on his sofa. It was close to the 24th Street BART station too, so if Bebe was being bitchy they could jump the gates and head somewhere else.

They had this thing for the place, aside from its handy conveniences (like a whole room that acted as a piss hole). The abandoned factory was a fog of dust, lath showing through crumbling holes like a whale's ribs, carpeting like the surface of a swamp. There was something about its decay and mold that always put them in a fucking mood to fuck.

Spike and Spike were tall and thin: They were skeletons dancing in bags of pale white skin, navels done (steel), eyebrows done (one gold, one steel), septum done (big steel), tats of primitive sunbursts around their right nipples, and PAs done (steel).

They were wild boys, feral kids. They had some money, just enough, but more important than cash or a place without rats to crash, they had each other.

Fuck that, they *were* each other. It was a damned art to them, to mix, merge, switch, combine, and, every chance they fucking got, to fraternize with each other. They weren't just twins—smiling goofs from some commercial. They were a young guy who happened to be in two places at once. It was a point of pride between Spike and Spike that they didn't use first names (tell one, tell both) and that no one (not even Spike and Spike) could tell which was who and who was which—just Spike, man, just Spike...

They took an extreme delight in their similarities, sharing everything with each other and trading back and forth so often that even in the rare instance of them being apart you could never, ever, be sure which one you were with. And it didn't matter because if you were with one today you would be with the other tomorrow.

Spike—kneeling at Spike's feet, mouth wide open to catch his hot jism, furiously working his own long, pale cock—was just about to crest. Nothing got Spike more worked up than tasting Spike's come. It got him so juiced, in fact, that he was way ahead of Spike on the ladder.

Spike could tell that his brother was going to beat him to the punch and come way fucking sooner than he was. Didn't seem right, Spike figured, for Spike to get so hot and come from just the idea of swallowing his milk, and not from swallowing him. Pissed, he reached down and grabbed Spike's head, impaling his thin, blood-red lips around his long, pale cock while skillfully kicking his brother's hands away from his throbbing dick.

Moaning at having his brother's long, thin cock down his throat, Spike swallowed and rolled his hard tongue around his brother's cock and locked his hands tight on the backs of his meaty thighs. Spike, meanwhile, groaned the good groan and lifted a leg over his brother's head—twisting around to show Spike his asshole and to reach down and lock a sweaty palm around Spike's pulsing, bobbing cock.

Gravity won in the end. As Spike reached for his brother's member, he lost his balance and collapsed on top of him into a natural, though slightly bruised, sixty-nine. Spike plunged his mouth onto his brother's cock just as, at the other end, the same was done to him.

Mouth/cock, cock/mouth, they moaned, sucked, and slobbered (it's really good when you don't care you're drooling) and rocked back and forth—feeling at the same time as sucking, sucking at the same time as feeling. Coming, like that, was one of the major things that kept them glued together as *Spike*.

They came together, or at least as close as they could get: Spike jetting into his brother's face, cock jerking as it spurted sticky come down into Spike's laughing face. Spike coming up toward his brother's also-smiling face. But his come's trajectory was different for being on the bottom and it splattered the plaster-dusted floor of their hideaway with a white abstract.

They broke for a moment, knocking back huge swallows of cheap white wine from a bag. Breathing heavily, they kissed, mixing salty protein and acid high with their steamy mouths. Quickly, their cocks again tapped at their legs and thighs. Also quickly, they stroked each other to an iron strength with the lube of their previous come.

Spike was the first to go down on Spike. Shoving his long, pale legs out from behind him he swallowed his brother's sword without a blink or even a hint of teeth or a bend of his throat. To Spike, receiving, it was dipping his cock in an intimate, hot tunnel that gripped him with all the dexterity of his own—or his brother's—hand.

Giving, Spike snaked a long-fingered hand down to his own cock and rolled over onto his side so he could stroke himself as he sucked off his brother.

On the good ride to a second come, Spike bent back, catching his rapid descent just in time with his hands. Now propped, he watched with sexy joy as his brother sucked him up and down and up and down—his shaft gleaming with spit and friction.

Then...it...happened.

Spike, the sucking, stuck a finger into the asshole of Spike, the sucked. Now it should be noted that Spike's asshole wasn't exactly what you'd call virgin territory. The act of having a finger eased into it, and him, wasn't—in itself—all that shocking. But what Spike did with it caused...well, wait: Spike stuck a finger into his brother's asshole as he sucked him off, a mad hydraulic machine. Then, with his finger deep in his brother's puckered hole, he swiped it around, relishing and playing with the contours of Spike's anus. Then he managed to get his finger just far enough inside to feel around for, then find, his magic button.

Maybe it was the quality of the blow job. Maybe it was the

surprising skill with which Spike found Spike's P spot, but whatever the cause, Spike came like crazy.

Then he got mad.

"Where the fuck did you learn that?" Spike said, standing, pulling his still-hard cock out of his brother's mouth with a cartoon *pop!*

Spike sat back and shrugged, his blond quills all but rattling on his head. "Dunno."

"*We* haven't done anything like that."

"Just thought it might feel good," Spike said, shyly, reaching again for his brother.

"Bullshit! You got that from someone else! Who have you been fucking?"

Spike smiled, this time slyly. "Fuck off."

"I will not fuck off! Who the fuck have you been fucking?"

Spike got to his feet. They were twins, each the same height as the other. Still, standing, Spike seemed to tower over his angry brother. "Fuck off! It isn't important."

"Fuck that shit! We're supposed to only fuck each other, right? Isn't that how it's supposed to work? You fuck me and I fuck you, right? So who else have you been fucking?"

Spike's reply was a clumsy but effective swing. Catching him in his pale stomach, Spike's fist knocked Spike off balance and he feel to his knees, clutching his shocked stomach, his throbbing muscles. Spike watched him, gagging and all but puking at his feet for a beat—two—then knelt and grabbed him by his short blond hair and lifted him a few inches. "I've been *fucking* bored!"

Spike obviously wasn't all that hurt. He stood and swung in one quick motion, aiming for his brother's jaw. But Spike was clearer-headed than his brother and saw the fist barreling at him as if in slow motion. One quick little dance step—plaster crackling underfoot—and Spike's straining fist shot by his ear. As Spike followed his flying fist, Spike slugged him again in the stomach.

Spike dropped to his knees, gagging and clutching his brother's thighs.

Looking down at his brother, Spike panted as well—but from exertion. His cock, he noticed suddenly, was as hard as a fucking rock and thumping firmly against the top of his brother's head. Reaching down, he grabbed Spike's hair and tilted his head just enough so that he was staring at it. "Suck. And make it good or I'll fucking kill you," he said, pulling Spike's head onto his cock.

Spike swallowed it, letting his brother pull his mouth, lips, and throat onto his burning hot cock. Spike had never seen his brother so hard before. Distantly, as he sucked and sucked, he was aware that his own cock was also rubber-wrapped iron, and that he'd started to stroke himself.

Moaning, Spike hauled his brother to his feet. "You're a fucking boring lay," he yelled into Spike's face, as spit rolled down his face. "Boring!" He slapped him, hard, and watched the skin of his lips and mouth vibrate with the impact. Spike whimpered, but his cock stayed hard.

"Boring!" *Slap!*

"Boring!" *Slap!*

A few drops of blood flecked the corner of Spike's mouth. Spike bent forward and kissed them off his brother, tasting copper and brine. Then he hit him again.

Spike grabbed his brother and spun him around threw him to the plaster-dusted boards. He landed hard, groaning as his hard cock slammed onto the floor with him. Spike knelt down quickly and wrapped a hard arm around his brother's waist and hauled him into a kneel. "*You're...*" he screamed, sure as shit someone would hear and come busting down the door "...*a fuck-ing*..." and come pouring in "...*boring fuck!*"

He slapped his brother across the ass, at first about as hard as he'd slapped his face and then, when Spike didn't even seem to notice, a lot harder.

Under him, Spike moaned. His juicy asshole puckered and relaxed with the anticipation of each impact that followed.

Spike's slaps became a to-and-fro applause: hitting one cheek on the fore swing and the other on the back. The sound rolled through the sad room, sounding like a standing ovation at the end of an opera. More so with the "*thankyouthankyouthanky-outhankyouthankyouthankyou...*" from Spike.

Spike, his ass turning redder and redder with each *slap*, start-ed to jerk and twitch with the impacts, bucking and humping his straining cock against a section of less-than-threadbare rug.

Spike's hand started to hurt, especially his fingertips—getting it from the backstroke. A lightbulb went on over his head and he reached to where their clothes lay in a denim-and-cotton heap and pulled loose his belt.

The sound was like a shot in the room, and Spike half expect-ed to see a window blow from the percussion. The heavy leather slammed into Spike's pink ass cheeks like a fist into a sandbag. Spike screamed, shrill and sharp, and tried to scoot away. Spike, though, reached a strong arm out, grabbed his ankle, hauled him back, and smacked him again and again with the belt.

Spike's screams turned into a long wail—a stuck siren—then melted into a stream of deep grunts. Spike's ass was cher-ry, glowing as if stoked by an internal fire. In a few places he'd even started to bleed: a few tiny cuts from the metal studs on Spike's heavy belt.

"Maybe the next time you'll try and be a bit more...*imagina-tive!*" Spike yelled, putting his back, shoulder, and whatever remained in his arm into five final swings. He watched, hypnotized and drunk with causing his brother so much enjoyable pain, as Spike's ass ate the blows with a heavy jiggle. Spike had progressed beyond moans and groans: He just hung his head down and roared.

Spike's cock was doing its own kind of aching. He was so horny his balls screamed *blue* as loud as they could. With a snap, he looped his belt around his brother's waist and hauled him up from his sprawl on the floorboards. He dropped to his knees and he pulled Spike's ass and asshole right onto his aching cock.

Spike's asshole just ate him up—swallowing him whole, drinking him down.

Spike and Spike had never been hotter, tighter, harder. They fucked like the real meaning of the word: hammering and getting hammered. They slammed into each other, fucker and fuckee, until they couldn't keep the stopper in anymore—Spike on the bottom jerking off in sync—Spike shooting onto the floorboards and his brother shooting into his ass.

Then they passed out, one on top of and still in, the other under, and still hard.

Later, afterward, Spike and Spike, identical twins, could be seen walking down the street, any street. No, that's a lie—merely a definition. Afterward, after that day in the barn (lie), they were not identical. It was easy to tell Spike from Spike.

Spike and Spike walking down the street: Spike leading Spike, towing him around by a chain, a leather thong, a cord, some rope, or just an ordering crook of a pale finger. He was always the Spike in control, the one with the gruff voice, the snap in his tone.

And behind him, there was the Spike that was always there, always smiling a satisfied smile, always the bottom.

After that day, you always knew Spike from Spike.

How Coyote Stole the Sun

The bus dropped to its knees, yawning open its door. The day was burning: the sun angry at something it wasn't sharing and the wind scared to come out.

Dust swirled, friendly and clinging, around Dog as he left the cooling bosom of the Interstate Lines bus. Satisfied that its friend was out and walking safely away, No. 47—Albuquerque to Taos, N.M.—closed its door and left with a belching cloud of exhaust.

The trees must have had issues with Dog, because as he approached them they shuffled and fluttered their leaves to flash pieces of the too-hot sun down on him.

But Dog was used to that kind of treatment from trees—he paid them no mind and just kept on walking along the dusty road.

After a time of walking—precisely how long being difficult to say because time wasn't something Dog really understood and because watches, as a group, refused to speak true to him—Dog saw signs of man: the broken teeth of a old picket fence, the rusting mesh of its chain-link brother, the stumps of telephone poles, and, distantly, the regularity of a small house.

A few steps later, details filled his eyes: It was a small house. Clapboard, painted red. A porch that was a mixture of rotting and rotted old boards. Glassless windows with torn curtains like pale moss. A screen door with more holes than screen.

It took Dog a few seconds to really see the two little boys, they were so faded into the grasses and the shadows. They were brown and furtive from running with the rabbits and the squirrels. Their eyes were as blue as the sky in a good mood, and as tame as wild foxes. They were naked and tanned—dirty and scuffed and uncaring, unworried. Maybe nine summers, maybe ten. Not 12. They could have been brothers or just kin playing outside together too long.

Dog watched them, doing nothing for a while, and then he dropped onto his haunches, feeling his old blue jeans creak and stretch against his thighs. Putting two fingers on the ground, he gave the boys the gift of thinking he needed the fingers for balance—when Dog could have stayed there for many nights without moving.

After a time, the two wild boys decided he wasn't a hunter, or at least not a hungry one. Cautiously, they came out from the high grasses in front of dead house and looked at him.

Finally, the one with echoes of being civilized, or just less of the music of the wild world, spoke: "What you doing here, mister?"

Dog answered, slowly and without threatening timbre, "Just passing."

The boy who spoke nodded, as if that was more than enough, or all he could understand.

Dog played a bit with the dust at his feet, careful to draw something without meaning. "Anything around here?" he said.

The other boy, the one who didn't speak, heard a sound and

leaped into the weeds in pursuit. The other looked like he wanted to join his friend or brother but was still too fascinated by the stranger. "Birds. Rabbits. Mice. Squirrels. Roc."

"Roc?"

The remaining boy jerked his head down the road. "He has more than anyone. Even stuff."

"Stuff?" Dog said, standing and brushing the clinging dust from his denim jacket.

The boy looked confused, as if he didn't have any other words. Another sound chirped from the high, brown grasses and he looked harder this time in its direction: The wild wasn't calling; it was screaming for his small attention.

He looked at Dog once more, decided he didn't have anything else to say, or that he lacked the means to say what he wanted, and bounded off into the grasses to make hunting and catching noises all his own.

Dog watched the grasses shake and shush, then turned and walked down the road.

Roc?

Once it was a town. Now, though, most of the houses, from lack of company or just uncaring company, were dead: Their doors hung loosely open, their only breaths a turgid breeze dancing among their corpses. Their paint was either faded or completely gone, showing dry boards and rotting wood.

The street was as unpaved as ever, with ruts like canyons from the breeze and occasional rains.

Dog saw four buildings: a grocery bare of life, a two-story hotel (Excelsior) with dead air as guests, a gas station fuzzy with weeds and grasses, and a garage.

The garage sat against a low hill fuzzy with dead yellow grass. A sickly oak shaded it. Like the others: peeling paint, empty-eyed windows, and rattling signs. But unlike the others the garage, with a sign reading YOU NEED IT/WE HAVE IT, had a clinging kind of life. The weeds in front were dead, but also cut back. The building, a Quonset hut, was tired, old, and cancered with pocks of rust, but it was organized: Crates of Coke, motor oil, K rations, rolls of chicken wire, and drums of gasoline were placed in clusters against it. Its dirty and dark windows seethed with a glowering intensity. The garage might still be alive, but it held its life close to its chest.

The sun was still pissed; it tried to cook Dog as he walked through the town, but Dog was used to this kind of treatment from the sun and so its harshness just rolled off his denim-covered back. Tipping his leather hat a bit lower over his eyes, he walked toward the garage.

Its door was open, cool air swirling out from the dark insides.

"Howdy," Dog said to the man inside.

Dog had seen no one else so far, so it must have be Roc, he thought. It must be Roc for other reasons too: His skin was heavy and granite; he was fat from storage of everything he could get; he bulged with selfish satisfaction, a statue carved from dark woods. Dressed in a simple pair of torn and faded denim overalls and sitting on a sagging stool with rollers, you could see, and Dog could see, that he was fat. But it was a strong kind of fat. Big, not blown out of perspective. Roc's skin was tan stretching to burnt black. His face, what Dog could see of it from a misty beam coming through one window of the garage, was strong and not jowly. He had a stone, cleft chin, and eyes that glimmered deep, deep blue. A gray and black mane of unkempt hair fell from the top of his head, stopping just short of his shoulders. The lines of his face, the planes and crags, told a tale of great strength, power, and a stern attitude toward survival. He was here, and he had what he needed to stay here. He lived to acquire and stay strong at all costs.

All from his body and face. That, and the back of the garage—a treasure throve of things: boxes of Rice Krispies, stacks of romance novels and *Playboy*s, drums of oil, tanks of propane, bundles of fishing poles, crates of lawn mowers, and piles of Gold Circle condoms.

Roc responded to Dog's greeting with a slow, tentative, guarded nod.

"Someone," Dog said, walking into the freezing shade of the doorway and leaning, oh-so-casual, against the roll-up door frame, "told me you might have some stuff."

"Could be." Roc's voice was deep and brass, as strong and big as his body. He didn't use it often, but when he did, everything with ears paid attention.

Dog knocked back his hat with a quick flick of his thumb and smiled with his eyes, if not his expressive mouth. "I might be interested in some stuff. Especially if you happen to have some, shall we say, special stuff."

"Could be," avalanches, thunderstorms, grinding equipment and mine shafts. "Could be."

"Not just what you might call ordinary special stuff. I speak of the *special* kind of special stuff. Unusual, more rare than ordinary *stuff*. YouknowwhatImean?"

Roc smiled, the planes and inclines of his great, ponderous face shifting into a shark's grin. "I know what you mean," he said, shifting his great body back and forth and tapping his thigh, indicating the presence of more rare than ordinary stuff under his ponderous ass.

Dog smiled his special smile, the one he reserved for virgins, for people who said they didn't play poker all that well, for double-

or-nothing, for "Do you love me?" and for "What you gonna do about it?" and said, "Now that, sir, sounds like exactly the kind of thing that someone like me just might be interested in."

Roc shook his granite head, dropped his own smile down to something that spoke *I'll break you in half,* and said, "Not for sale."

"I can understand that, sir, I really can. I'm a man of the world, you understand. I'm a fella who knows what you mean, knows this isn't what you would call a negotiable point. I can hear that, sir, I know that tune. I'm not one of those who would press you on this thing. I'm not one of those who'd insult you by pulling a great wad of money out of his back pocket and dropping it casual on the ground with the kind of understanding, unspoken of course, that if you were to, say, get up and come over and pick it up that that would be an invitation to come over there and pick up that special *stuff* and be on my way."

"No," said Roc simply.

"I understand, sir, I really do. Like I said, I'm not one of those who would make such an offer to a fella like you. I'm not that kind, I assure you. I'm not one of those who would tell you he happens to know a certain young lady in a nearby town, a young pump of a girl, you might say. A certain lady who could, and would, for a special friend of mine, do things with her bee-sting lips, her strong, round ass, her cushy pussy, that would make your eyes melt right in your head, sir."

"No."

"I'm not that kind, sir, like I said. I'm not even the kind who would simply leave it hanging, implying there might be something I could give you that would make you get off the most-comfortable looking chair and therefore give me this most special stuff."

Roc was as quiet as his spiritual brothers. He sat in the cool semi-darkness and stared at the relaxed figure of Dog leaning against the door frame. Time, as was said, wasn't something reliable around Dog, but it was some number of those flighty things called seconds, those quick things called minutes, and maybe even one of those heavy things called hours before he said, "Maybe."

Dog smiled. This one was his special smile, the one he kept in his back pocket and only took out when someone said "Maybe."

"I'm not the kind of fella," Dog said, pushing himself gently away from the door and walking into the cool dimness of the garage, "who might take that as a guarantee or something. It's just potential, right? It's just that we have opened what you might call *lines of communication.* We have something to talk about. We know that I might be able to offer you something that might be attractive enough to make you rise from that very comfortable-looking stool and therefore offer me your special stuff. Potential, that's all."

"Right," said Roc, eyes gleaming like polished steel. "We can talk."

"Yes we can, great Roc. We can. Maybe, sir, I should start by stating that I have many talents, many skills, innumerable resources at my disposal. I have many things to offer, Roc, many things that might *interest* you." Dog walked deeper into the dim chill of the garage, walking on the dirt floor until he was just a dozen hands away from the giant man.

Almost invisibly, Roc smiled.

Dog smiled too: *that* smile again. The knowing grin, a curling of the lips and a slight flash of white, sharp teeth that said *I see you clearly now.*

And Roc smiled because he saw Dog clearly now, too—a tall, lanky man filling a pair of jeans with muscles. Denim jacket and stained T-shirt promising broad shoulders and a strong chest. Dirty, battered hat. Dog looked like many, but with an added extra that made people and things like the wind and the sun watch him walk by. His face was rugged and unshaven, wind-sculpted and tanned to the point of leather. His nose was long and sharp, announcing the man before his true arrival. His eyes were shaded by a heavy tangle of brow. His lips were chapped and coarse, though full and broad around a large mouth. His face was tough and used, but held a mirthful experience: What Dog had been through hadn't hardened him as much as filled him. He had seen a lot of this, you could tell, and that, and it had all made him smile. From wisdom or from blind stupidity, though, it was very hard to tell.

"Anything at all that might interest you. Maybe some kind of task I might perform? Now, without beating my own...drum so to speak, might I propose some kind of...test of strength, perhaps, or endurance, or performance, maybe—something along those lines? May I be so bold?"

Inside the shaded, cool garage it was remarkably hard to see and know for sure—but Dog's eyes had adjusted from the pounding of the sun outside to the dimness inside—but a smile seemed to have crept across Roc's adamantine face. Were those the yellow tombstones of his teeth? Dimples? Hard to say.

The garage was quiet. The only sound came from the gentle breezes playing outside, rattling loose windows and rocking empty oil drums back and forth. Dog's hearing was sharper than most, more acute—he could tell which of those gusts playing outside was male and which was female—and so he could pick up words where others wouldn't have.

"Pick me up," he heard, spoken very softly. Inaudible to anyone but Dog. And even Dog wouldn't have been sure if he hadn't seen Roc's lips move.

Dog smiled and bowed deep, so deep that the tip of his battered hat actually touched the dust and dirt floor of the garage.

"Most humble Roc. I cannot begin to tell you how pleased you have made me by giving me this most challenging of tasks." Then, as if he suddenly realized what he had said, he quickly added, amended: "Not to imply in any way that you are of unnatural girth, kind sir. Not at all. I, for instance, have laid eyes on many more giant specimens of man. I have seen many others much more huge, much more grotesquely magnificent in their dimensions. You, in fact, are svelte in comparison to some of these grander gentlemen."

This time, for sure, Roc smiled. And this time, for sure, Roc spoke, gravel tumbling in a steel drum: "Pick me up," he said again. "*Now.*"

"I will most humbly attempt to perform this task," Dog said, standing and moving toward and then around the huge man.

Carefully, craftily, Dog inspected Roc. He saw what he saw the first time, but this time with greater detail that closer range brought: the brass buttons on the giant fellow's overalls straining in their reinforced loops, the tanned-to–deep brown skin, the valleys and broad plateaus of Roc's well-defined muscles. Yes, he was big. Yes, he was huge. But it was the kind of size that doesn't come from excess; it was a size of natural dimensions. Roc was big, but also strong.

"This could be quite a challenge," said Dog, slowly circling Roc, running his thin, long fingers over the taut skin and tight denim. He let his fingers fall into the creases, tracing definitions he'd seen with his eyes. "Not to say that you are too big to even contemplate moving."

Roc's laugh was thunder rolling over high hills, an earthquake, a tide retreating from a rocky beach. There was a smile in his words: "Pick me up if you can."

Dog make a sneezing *here goes* sound and said: "Very well, kind and gentle and rather, very, extremely, incredibly, *big* Roc. I will attempt to lift you bodily from your perch and hoist you onto my shoulder."

Roc laughed again.

Dog found a place behind Roc, where his huge ass made two great globes of muscle around the tiny roller chair on which he was perched. Making a grandiose show of spitting into his hands and bending his legs and cracking his back, Dog put one hand on each side of the huge man and breathed deep and hard.

Roc, with the contact, tensed as if a minor jolt of current had been unleashed—feeling the strength in Dog's arms, the warmth of his breath on the small of his back. Dog's hands were iron on his sides and chest.

"Ready, big man?" Dog said, from behind.

Roc nodded, and Dog's breathing increased. Then, he lifted.

Roc felt himself lose weight through the strength of Dog. Under him, the chair creaked. He felt the sudden shift of his overalls, his ankles leave the metal of the chair struts, and his back realign.

Behind him, lifting, Dog was vibrant force: the ground, the sky, the wind. Roc felt the strength of Dog, the power of the man, and it excited him: His cock strained, mighty and mighty hungry, against the thickness of his overalls.

Dog wheezed and strained, panted and heaved. Distantly, both of them heard and both of them felt Dog's back give a little pop of strain.

Almost, almost, almost...

Then Roc's weight returned. The chair and on it the container of stuff creaked and groaned. Roc felt his weight return to its normal broadness against the seat. In a moment he was back to his usual distribution of self.

"My most humble, profound, extreme, sincere, earnest (pant, heave, pant, heave) apologies, Roc," Dog said, his breath steamy against Roc's broad back where he rested his face. "But this seems to be beyond my humble ability. I am so sorry. Is there anything else I might do for your magnificence that might facilitate me receiving the stuff in your possession?"

Roc smiled, though Dog couldn't see it.

In the garage, with the wind rattling gentle at the windows, Roc's voice was shockingly strong and loud: "Empty me."

Dog, still gently wheezing from the exertion of trying to lift the massive Roc, came around to the front of the huge man. Dog was smiling: a wicked and pleased smile that stretched from slightly pointed ear to slightly pointed ear. "It would be the humblest of pleasures, dear, kind, huge, Roc, to be the recipient of you, to swallow you until only the barest of you remains. It will be my pleasure to drain you of your sweetest stuff, to sup you of your delicious nectar."

Roc's mammoth hands left his lap where they had been calmly folded, and with glacial slowness undid the top right, then top left buttons of his overalls. Thick denim fell to his sculpted belly. The material fell into a faded apron over the mound of Roc's belly, and he took his big left hand and dug down below his waist.

Dog had seen bigger cocks for sure. On whales, definitely. On elephants, positively. On bears, rhinos, panthers and tigers and pumas and cougars and moose and that guy, Lou, who worked in a gas station in Memphis—but this one was damned close to huge. It was so damned close to positively huge that Roc had a hard time freeing it from his overalls. When he finally did, after much slow fumbling, his cock pointed up, right up, at Dog.

Roc was uncut, his foreskin as tanned and dark as the rest of his teak skin. The shaft was like...many things—a baseball bat, a fence post, an arm, a leg—and it was lovely, strong, and powerful. Its veins and muscles played and danced with the contractions of excitement along its length, making the massiveness of it bob up and down. Dog knew he would from then on be comparing all those things—fence posts and baseball bats and arms and legs—to Roc's cock, and not the other way around.

The base of Roc's massive cock was buried in a forest primeval of curly, stiff hairs. His balls, what Dog could see of them, were the size of baseballs, apples...no: Apples, oranges, baseballs, peaches, and pears were the size of Roc's lovely balls.

Obviously, Roc was happy with his cock, and with Dog: A thick droplet of creamy precome dotted the end and, as Dog looked from it to Roc's stern and (maybe) slightly smiling stone face, the drop fell with a weighty plop to the dirt floor.

"I shall," Dog said, stricken to short sentences by the sight of Roc's member, "endeavor to accomplish."

On his knees on the dirt floor, Dog kissed and cleaned the foreskin with his soft, soft tongue, licking all around the base of the head, tasting the sweat and manliness of the cock, feeling the corona through the thick skin, and then, finally—with a groan from Roc—he put his full lips on the tip and gently swallowed the thick bead that swelled there.

Slowly, Dog opened his mouth wider and wider until his teeth were oh-so-gently tapping against the ridge of the hidden cock head. Then, with his strong and supple lips—as well as his learned and maneuverable tongue—Dog slowly pushed himself onto Roc's cock.

In Dog's wide open mouth, Roc's cock was a stone covered in silk—a great weight perfectly formed into the head of a cock. The foreskin peeled back, retracting smooth and supple until the bare cock head filled Dog's soft mouth.

Above Dog, Roc permitted himself a subterranean growl that vibrated through his body and dribbled a thimbleful of come down the back of Dog's throat.

Then Dog really started to work.

First he bathed Roc's cock head with his tongue, teasing and milking it. To Roc, it felt like both a mouth and a hand were working him, drawing the come and the come juice out like a snake charmer at work.

In fact, the music of Dog's blow job was so skilled and so well orchestrated that Roc soon felt his great reservoir of come start to boil and seethe with an impending orgasm.

Then it was too late. The fuse (in Dog's mouth) burst into pleasurable, throbbing sparkles, racing down and through the shaft of Roc's cock and straight into his belly and balls. There, the gates were opened and his juice roared out and into Dog's hungry mouth.

Cups? Pints? Gallons? Hard to say, but whatever the immense amount, Dog gulped and swallowed and consumed every last bit, letting it flow down his throat and into his belly. Above him, Roc flowed rivers of sweat and groaned and moaned and cried with the power of his come. He seemed to deflate, to diminish as his juice flowed out of him.

Dog swallowed it all—save a last tiny bit, which flowed over Dog's lips and splashed onto the dirt floor.

"My apologies. My most humble, humble apologies, great and powerful Roc," said Dog, standing and wiping his mouth, chin, and face with a large red handkerchief. "I am most ashamed that again I have disappointed your huge and magnificent self with my poor performance of the task you have set before me. I can only hope that you will look back on this, and me, kindly and not with scorn, and—"

"Shut up," Roc said, hugely, "and fill me."

That smile again. "Sure," Dog said.

Walking behind the great mountain, Dog played his hands along the broad, strong back of Roc, among the valleys and ranges, feeling and then tasting the torrents of sweat trickling off the huge man.

Roc pulled his overalls further down to expose his asshole.

Despite his worldly experience, Dog looked and whistled: puckered mouths, rose blossoms—all now would be compared to the asshole of Roc. For such a huge man, Roc had a surprisingly dainty asshole. Well, not exactly dainty—Roc's asshole was easily the size of a half-dollar, and firm and tight and pink and clean—more like "cute." Though if Dog had said as much, he was sure he would have been squished like jam between bricks by the massive hands of Roc.

Instead, he said, "I will strive to accomplish this more pleasurable of tasks, this plumbing of your most intimate depths, the filling of your aching emptiness with my most humble of—"

Roc inhaled, as if ready to speak his rumbling tones.

"I'm doing it, I'm doing it!" Dog said, fumbling with his belt. When his jeans dropped to the dirt floor they kicked up tiny clouds of yellow dust that, as friendly as their outside counterparts, clung to Dog's hairy legs.

Dog's own member was much more...sedate than Roc's, of much more modest proportions and dimensions. When one viewed, and many had done so, Dog's penis, the things that came to mind were of a much humbler variety: flashlights, ears of corn, zucchinis, and the like.

Still, even though it was a bit smaller than the giant's, Dog's cock had a lot of character. His was a cock that spoke of wild fucks, mad fucks, quick fucks, fucks in strange and weird places, of assholes, mouths, melons, fists, and the occasional cunt. It was long and tapering, uncut like Roc's, but bent in a curious way—down and to the left—and the head was bulbous and nicked by scars, as if maybe one or more recipient had been alarmed by Dog's use of it.

"I will," sighed Dog, stroking his cock to a righteous state of iron readiness, "endeavor to perform this task."

And with that, he spat into his hand and lubed Roc's asshole, which, being an obviously well-trained asshole, immediately bloomed open around his gentle fingers.

When Roc's back door was quite ready, willing, and more than likely able, Dog carefully positioned himself so the head of his cock was resting gently against Roc's pucker, and grabbed hold of Roc's strong sides.

"Ready?" he inquired in excited tones.

No sound came, but the giant head nodded.

As asshole fucks go, the one between Dog and Roc that day wasn't the absolute. Some others could have exceeded it in terms of length of time, intensity, passion, determination, depth, and resulting orgasm—but none came to mind.

For Roc, the slender wanderer's cock was an iron shaft gliding in and out of his most tender and excited opening. The long and strong shaft reached in and tickled and fucked him in ways he'd never experienced. After a few minutes, Dog's skillful use of his cock inside him had started the engine of his come. Great rivers of sweat poured off him and his eyes fluttered with the anticipation of an mind-altering orgasm.

For Dog, Roc was the perfect thing to fuck: big and wide and hot and tight and lubed and eager. His asshole was an amusement park of sensation and pressure. His skilled tissues felt like hands, tongues, and lips, all striving to push him up and over the top.

When they met at the peak of their respective comes, the orgasms that rocked and rolled through the two of them were sticks of lit dynamite. Dog exploded with a spasming jerk, as if live wires had been grounded in his arms and legs. Roc felt as if molten lead had been squirted into his tender asshole.

Dog filled Roc with his come, almost all the way, but then...

Dog's legs gave out. Dropping back onto his bare ass on the

dirt floor, he jetted a last pint or so into the air and all over his shirt. "You have (pant) my ultimate (sigh) forgiveness, great and mighty (wheeze) Roc, for I have failed again in my attempt at the task you have set before me."

Roc didn't say anything, didn't do anything but sit on his tiny, wheeled chair and pant and wheeze and gasp.

Staggering to his feet, Dog dusted his ass off and hitched up his battered jeans, saying all the while: "I feel so bad, great Roc, for failing you in not one, not two, but three of the tasks you have set before me. I feel so inadequate as a man and a being that I do not think I can even raise my head again. I can never meet the eyes of another knowing I have failed you in these tasks. I feel I can never redeem myself for these failures...

"Unless," Dog added, and there was that smile again, "I might attempt one of these tasks again, say. Another, no doubt, fruitless attempt at something you know I have already dismally avoided success in. Maybe then I might be able to restore my sense of pride in myself and my abilities as a man."

Now it should be said that two orgasms (like trains entering tunnels) had already had their way with the giant Roc, and that he had few brain cells that were actually working at that time. It was expected, then, that the only thing that did come to mind for him was either once again having Dog's lovely mouth and throat on his cock or having Dog's incredible cock inside him. With his functioning brain cells, Roc said, "Sure. (wheeze) Anything."

So Dog smiled that smile again and grabbed Roc around his huge middle and lifted his now very diminished, shrunk, and exhausted form off the stool. While he wheezed and panted and strained again, it was obviously easier this time—Roc was just light enough to do it. Held high, Dog kicked out with his right foot and neatly booted the "stuff" off the stool, sending it skidding across the floor of the garage.

Then he dropped Roc back onto his stool and sprinted like a wild animal around Roc's flailing arms—like whirling stone paddles—scooped up the stuff, neatly contained in a battered and stained Sucrets box, and ran for the door.

Where he stopped, turned, bowed deep, and said, "It was indeed a great pleasure meeting you and taking your stuff, Mr. Roc."

Then he turned and left, leaving the bellowing Roc behind.

Down the road, by the house, Dog stopped a moment to heave and pant and wheeze some more, bracing himself against one of the rotten fence posts. Satisfied that Roc was completely unwilling or unable to follow him, Dog allowed himself yet another special smile—one that said *Got ya!*—and decided to look at his prize.

The little metal box was quite stubborn, but he finally managed to pry it open and look inside.

A mirror. Reflected in the mirror was the sun, burning hot and dry and mean over his head.

Curious, dumbfounded, and more than a little pissed, Dog turned the box this way and that, trying to puzzle it out. He did this for many minutes until, at last, he shrugged his shoulders as he done many times before and would do many times again, and chucked the box over the broken fence and into the weed-choked yard.

Then he left, humming absently to himself.

A short time later, the boys found the box among their weeds and took it with them. A little time after that, they thanked the lanky stranger who had come and gone—leaving them such an incredible gift.

The Harley

If they'd thought of B.O., Mammoth would have kicked it over and tore out of there no problem. Hands down, the fucker had the most righteous stench—one like a rap sheet (fucking bad and sticks to your ass for life): body reek, oil, farts, old blood, dog shit—the works. But they didn't think of stink to settle the issue.

Now Monster, he would have won an ugly contest. Not that Mammoth was a dreamboat or anything—teeth like a shook-up graveyard, skin like a back road, nose like something grown from compost, hair a dry brush fire of greasy yellow just waiting for a match. Ugly as fucking hell, man, but fucking gorgeous standing next to Monster.

Bald dome scaly like an alligator with hives, mouth crooked with zigzagged old scars, beard a moth-eaten rug of steel brushes sloppily put together under a flat and wheezing nose. And those eyes, like two smoking sulfur matches floating in ripe piss or gasoline. Like most of them, Monster got yanked by the law a lot. Fuck, attitude alone (which stunk as much as Mammoth's pits) got him flashed and pulled over. He rarely got booked or nothin', though—most just yanked his chain till they saw those two match heads get struck by some interior spark, then they swallowed their last meal that'd come up on them quick-like and just let him be.

But they didn't think of ugly to settle the contest over the Harley.

It was a fair draw for reps, as it ended up. But any ol' fucker knows that ain't a way to settle this that kinda shit: Bullshit walks, right? Ain't no crazy motherfucker gonna say where and how much to anyone save his brothers—and then it's mostly bullshit anyway. Did anyone fuckin' see you cave that cop's dome by the Thrifty Mart? Fuck no. Did anyone see you blast through TJ with ten keys of pure shit? No, but everyone's heard you fucking did so shut the fuck up about it, all right? Yeah, we've all heard it, fuck-er, about how you fucked that frat boy up the ass back behind Greenie's pool hall with your ten-inch dick.

You can't count reps in this kinda thing. Especially with a couple of cast-iron pig fuckers like Mammoth and Monster. Two legends ain't gonna sit around no dried-up waste of asphalt back by the Mosco's Speed Track throwing back and forth: "I killed this dude, fucked this many, scored this, wasted that." Ain't that kind of scene with those kind of fuckers. Mammoth and Monster just stood and stared, scratched, flexed while Mammoth's Pup, perfect pale ass glowing in the track lights like a low, full moon, pissed like a racehorse into the mostly dead mesquite bushes as they tried to decide who'd get Bull's damned bike.

They didn't think of size, didn't toss it out like they'd tossed the other ideas out in two or three rumbling growls. Mammoth big. Pure big. Absolute big. Very, very, very fucking big—in three dimensions. No one called him fat, but that's what some thought seeing him sitting around his hog. Mammoth was big up and down and sideways—straining and stretching his colors and chaps, filling them with muscles laid on muscles. Mammoth wasn't a mountain as much as a boulder. Hands like outfielder's gloves, feet like phone books, head like a wrecking ball.

Monster was huge. They probably weighed the same: Mammoth big all around, Monster a skyscraper.

Birds had a tendency to fly around Monster. They came in all peaceful and calm and then screeched, banking when they saw that something tall and ugly had violated their airspace. When folks, civilians especially, saw Monster among his club they thought for maybe a beat, maybe a second, that he rode with fucking midgets. Maybe they'd smile, maybe they'd start to say something—but then they'd see, really see, that the rest of them were fucking big on their own, so that must mean that Monster was really, really...

...then they'd piss in their pants.

They didn't race for the bike, for Bull's prize Harley, 'cause they fucking already had. Two calls had been made when Bull had finally kicked after taking that bad spill on I-5. Everyone knew Bull had this cherry Harley sitting in his garage, knew that Bull rode with both Mammoth and Monster, knew those two fuckers hated lots of shit in this life but above all else each other, and fucking God and all his fucking angels knew that Bull just loved, fucking loved, to cause shit.

No surprise at all that Bull's old lady would make two calls right after Bull got planted in his backyard. Something like "It's yours if you haul ass down here right now."

No fucking surprise at that. Big fucking surprise that both of those mean and ugly assholes got there together.

Pup finished his Olympic piss and hiked his jeans, bored as all shit that they still couldn't decide how to see who'd get the bike.

"Jesus fucking Christ," he said, drifting all light and wispy-like over to Mammoth and running his soft hands down

Mammoth's jungle of scratchy chest hairs and around the peaks of his leathery nipples. "Someone fucking die already, man. I wanna get out of this fucking shit hole."

Lots of stuff said about the two of them, of Mammoth and Monster; lots even certified by law enforcement—usual and unusual—armed robbery, assault, battery, rape, possession, and possession to sell (usual); murder, assault on a police officer, transportation of illegal animal parts, bestiality, and suspected necrophilia (unusual). Cannibalism, as far as anyone really knew, was just a rumor. Both of them were like fucking storm fronts— tracked with precision by badges, rivals, and even their own clubs. There was even some bucks being shoved back and forth among riding "weathermen" to make sure the right kind of folks knew that the winds were just right or that one of the fucking hurricanes was bearing down on their vicinity.

Mammoth was an animal: He lived down deep with his wild urges, sharing space with all the old critters other folks might have fucking left behind. Folks may have been wild once, may have gone extinct in most, but Mammoth, though he was like, frozen in fuck- ing ice when the rest of us were in school. He runs wild and free, feasting on the little folks who forgot that maybe we used to feel the same way. Mammoth likes it fresh and red and hot. He likes to sleep after and laugh and howl during. He didn't fight so much as explode. He just recently stopped biting as much as he used to.

Now Monster, he wasn't so much wild as thoughtful. The call of the wild didn't ring for him—rather, he was more of an intel- lectually ugly motherfucker. Rumor was—and rumors were all you could hear because no one, no one, was talking—Monster was always the real ugly sort, but was only on the outside till he was able to hear what folks were saying about his face, his size. Then he sort of took it to heart, started trying it on for size. Monster cultivated himself, they said. He measured, tested, and refined it till people never, ever said anything except for fucking "Sir!" to his face.

Lots about those two. Some about Bull's legendary prize Harley: the special one, the real good one. All original, cared for like only Bull could care for a machine. It cranked like a dream, growled like feeding time at the zoo, and could out race a rep across the country.

But man, there was shit little about Pup.

Yeah, yeah, yeah—rumors. Always fucking rumors: the ex-cop, the ex-priest, the governor's son, the musician, and even the fucking astronaut. The best of them all, the ones not quite as big as Pup himself, said that sometime in the dim and distant (which wasn't that far back) past Pup used to live in this placed called the Castro, used to work in this little place called Fashion Flowers (decorator orchids), used to wear a fucking lot of taupe sweaters and listen to a fucking lot of ABBA—till his little blond head got turned by a persuasive ass fucking from a member of the Aces. From there he got passed around and around, not really a member of any club but more like a prize to be won. By 21 he was the Oscar for Most Vicious Motherfucker In Five States. Not only worth it, he was proud to be. Or so the rumors said.

He was Pup, and the one thing that was an absolute proven fact about the kid was that he could pull gas out of a bike without a hose.

"Look, bitch," Pup said to Mammoth (the only one, only one, who could say that to him), "it's getting fucking dark and my cock's gonna fall off. Will somebody please kill somebody so we can get the fuck out of here, OK?"

"Makes a lot of noise, don't he?" Monster said, leaning big and dark in shadows thrown from the track a hundred or so feet away. With a pop, the tall biker tipped a kitchen match off his thumbnail into brilliant flame and lit a fat cigar.

Mammoth snorted like he'd gotten stuck in tar or something and belched affirmative. "Does like to squeal a bit, he does."

"I'm fucking freezing my dick off here," Pup complained, hopping from one booted foot to the other, hugging himself while panting fading clouds of breath. "I want to get the fuck out of here."

"Shut the fuck up," Mammoth grumbled like rocks spilling from the top of a mountain. "I want the fucking bike, asshole."

"As do I," said Monster from the growing darkness, a toke of his cigar lighting his face like a red footlight.

"Well, I want to get the fuck out of here. I don't give a bleeding rat's ass about some motherfucking bike!"

"It's Bull's Harley," Mammoth said as if someone had questioned the color of the sun or the quality of Red Rose speed.

"It's prime," Monster said, agreeing with Mammoth for probably the first time ever.

"It's fucking cold, you cocksuckers. It's just a fucking bike, man. Can't it wait till fucking morning?"

"What does it take to shut him up?" Monster said, walking with earthquake steps from the dark into the brilliance cast by one of the racetrack lights.

"The usual," Mammoth said, smiling a flash of crooked yellow teeth as he levered himself off his bike and grabbed Pup by the shoulder.

"Aw, man, leave it, will ya? I want to fucking warm up already, OK?" Pup said, with a little less nelly in his voice, a tad more reason.

"Man don't know when to fucking quit," Monster said, close enough for Pup to get a face full of cigar smoke.

Between them, caught between the stogie and Mammoth's stink, Pup gagged and coughed a sudden cloud of breath. "Christ, give a fucking guy a break."

With a practiced move, Mammoth grabbed Pup's shoulder and jerked him around so he was facing the boulder biker. "The trick, man, is to just keep him to fucking busy," he said, shoving Pup down to the asphalt with a creak and pop of his joints.

"You motherfucker," Pup started, trying to get back up.

"Yeah, shithead," Mammoth said, popping his Harley belt buckle and unzipping his fly with one skilled tug. "Me motherfucker, you cocksucker."

They didn't think of cock size to settle the issue of Bull's bike. Maybe they didn't want to have it out, maybe didn't want their legends possibly...diminished in such a manly way. Maybe they just didn't have a reason to haul them out—yet.

As tall as he was around, Mammoth's cock wasn't: For such a bear, he had a snake's cock. In the hard glare of the lights from the track his dick was like a fucking pool cue sticking out of his pants. Mammoth's dick looked like it had been cleaned, polished. White and long, uncut head making it even more like a fucking spear or something, it leapt from his jeans like it got thrown from Mammoth's crotch towards Pup's mouth, like it fucking naturally lived in the kid's throat and Mammoth just kept it on a leash in his pants. The fucking ten inches wanted—wanted, man—Pup's lips and throat. Wanted it hard and wanted it bad.

"Oh, geez," Pup said, putting a hand around Mammoth's mammoth and stroking it like you might polish a brass horn, "no one fucking rides for free."

Lips to cock, with a mighty roar of one the racers on the track nearby as fucking applause, Pup got right down to it.

Now you might expect that taking in something like Mammoth's cock would take some practice, right?—even for a righteous cocksucker like Pup. Fact is, man, Pup is what Pup fucking does—got it? He sucks cock. He polishes, licks, kisses, swallows, works men's tools. Some men, they say, just have a clear purpose in life. Mammoth, now, he stinks—in body and fucking attitude. Monster is the perfect bogeyman, the stuff of cop nightmares, homeowner terrors, and mothers' horrors.

Pup, like I said, sucks.

Like drinking a glass of water, Pup opened his mouth and swallowed Mammoth's cock straight down. Could swear, man, that his teeth didn't even touch his meat—just straight fucking down. Ever see, reader, a snake swallow a chicken's egg? Just like that, friend, just like that: Jaws real, real far apart, Pup just tilted himself back and let it glide smooth and quick in his mouth and down his throat. Just as you'd think he'd start coughing or puking he just gave this little swallow, like, and took it all the way down.

"There," Mammoth said, "nice and quiet."

Soon, though, Mammoth wasn't. Even in the dim lights that spilled and splashed from the racetrack, Monster could see that were was some fancy throat work going on there between Pup's tonsils and Mammoth's cock: Like that snake swallowing that fucking egg, Pup started to work and pump and milk Mammoth's cock from down deep in his throat.

First Mammoth started to groan, then he started to whistle and mumble over and over, "motherfuckermotherfuckermotherfucker..." Soon he was grunting like a hog, howling like a wolf, and snorting like a bull.

Monster watched, at first detached, but then with sly interest, at Pup sucking Mammoth's cock. He watched quite intently, and maybe a little hungrily, till this kind of lightbulb went off over his head and he said, grinning from ear to hideous ear, "Pull out motherfucker. I got me a concept."

Mammoth pulled his dick out of Pup's magic mouth like a cork coming out of a bottle, the sharp pop! making Mammoth grin ear to ear. "Speak your mind," he said, adjusting his now–wet and dripping dick so his balls wouldn't scrape on his zipper.

Monster dropped down to one knee, grabbed Pup by his long blond tresses and tilted his head back, back. Pup squealed, more than likely with delight, and whimpered when Monster said into his dainty ears, "You like to make noise, right?"

At first, Pup started to nod, but found himself locked in the iron of Monster's grimy hand. So, instead, he swallowed, loud and liquid, and said, "Yeah, I do."

"Good," Monster said, suddenly letting go and leaving Pup to fall with a slap of denim onto the asphalt as Monster stood up. To Mammoth he said, "Man he makes the most noise for wins the bike."

Mammoth thought some time about this, working his great lantern jaw with a huge hand as he did so, as if the action somehow aided his reason. "Why the fuck not?" he said with a broad smile that showed off his jumble of teeth to their worst in the hard lights of the track.

"Call it, motherfucker," Monster said, pulling a quarter out of his pocket and flipping it high and sparkling into the track lights. Just before it landed, Mammoth said, "Heads." It dropped down into Monster's great hand (looking like a dime laying there), who then slapped it on his greasy and tanned arm.

Monster lifted his arm. The tiny head of Washington blinked up at them from a jungle of tangled arm hairs. "Heads it is."

"Right, motherfucker. Eat my dust," Mammoth said with a typhoon laugh, pulling his pants down. Bobbing from his scrub of dark public hairs, his cock bobbed and swung as if it had been cored with rebar. Still wet and shining from a few minutes down Pup's throat, Mammoth's cock was a bright pink, almost a sunburned red, and it bent up at a steep angle and slightly to the right. Down in the dark squiggles of his crotch, Mammoth's balls looked like hairy billiard balls in thick, wrinkled leather, and Monster, looking on with macho indifference, could almost imagine them banging together like the cue ball into the eight ball.

"On your feet, hole," Mammoth said, grabbing Pup and hauling him up by the front of his T-shirt till Pup was standing on the scuffed tips of his boots.

"I'm on them, I'm on them. Fuck!" Pup said, squeaking out from under the less-than-clean cotton fabric as Mammoth snapped his belt apart and jammed Pup's jeans down to his boots. No underwear. Not even a hard dick—yet.

"Assume the fucking position," Mammoth said with laughter in his thundering voice as he spun Pup around and jerked him down again, hard, till the blond boy was on his knees again but facing away from the mountain in denim.

"What the fuck do you think you're...Jesus!" Pup said, startled into a shrill squeal by the iron of Mammoth's cock stabbing into his back. "Look, let me get fucking ready at least. Fuck!" This time it was the same brilliant, red, long, thin cock thrusting into his coccyx. "At least hit the fucking...Christ!"

In.

Not fast. Sure as shit not easy, and fucking, fucking, fucking not fun—for Pup. Watching from the other side, all Monster could see was Mammoth's straining, muscular bulk moving with very precise twitches as he stuck his cock around Pup's ass then— as he sighted down his shaft with the nerves in his cock head—he jerked himself forward with perhaps (near as Monster could tell) half of his cock length.

Pup screamed, drowning out for a second the revving engines of the nearby race. The sound was sharp and high, the pain of Mammoth's iron jamming into his dry and pert asshole squealing out of him like toothpaste from a tube.

Mammoth pulled out and went in even harder.

Pup's cry cut like a sudden draft of freezing air around them, chilling Monster for a moment despite his size and sweating interest in Pup's getting fucked. After, though, after the scream was fading into the now-dark night, Pup's sounds became more guttural, more visceral: With another pump from Mammoth his scream faded into a throbbing grunt and didn't match Mammoth's thrusts with his huge hips.

Pup's face also went from wide and contorted to a softening mask of forced, closed eyes, bitten lips, and puffed cheeks. As Monster watched, his own cock hardening in his tight jeans, Pup started to moan and cry in a tempo that slowly started to approach the bucking of Mammoth behind him. His arms started to shake, and he started to droop and drop with each slamming blow of Mammoth's hips from behind him.

Pup's lips started to blow and hiss, but alternatingly smiled and gasped in swells and surges of butt-fucked pleasure. Despite an image and rep far more immense and powerful than he was, Monster was enraptured by Pup's face as he got fucked by the stroking engine of Mammoth's cock. Before he could think the usual, automatic biker *If I do this will I still be cool?* Monster knelt down to stare into Pup's playing, rippling face: pain, pleasure, pain, pleasure.

Carefully, Monster put a cigar-sized finger in front of Pup's mouth and groaned himself, earthquake and passing train, as Pup's eyes snapped open and he gently wrapped lips as smooth as fine silk around his walnut-sized knuckles and began to carefully suck.

This obviously was something that Mammoth didn't care for, because once he figured out that his rival for Bull's Harley was getting his finger worked, he really started to buck: he wasn't just fucking Pup, he was slamming, colliding with his ass. Butt fuck? No. Butt fucking? Damned straight.

And damned straight that Pup screamed again—high and shrieking, like Mammoth's cock had grown ten times and barbed as well. He fucking screamed like his asshole was getting cored. His mouth opened so wide and full that Monster was surprised that he didn't chomp down on his thick and callused finger.

But Pup didn't bite him. Didn't once. In fact, after the pain seemed to fade into merely unbearable, Pup started to work Monster's finger again: gentle, gentle, gentle.

Behind them, a train with its brakes burned off, Mammoth chugged and pistoned faster and faster down that highway that led to "I'm fucking coming!"

Then he fucking did, jerking and snapping this way and that like his own dick had gotten wrapped in barbed wire somewhere inside Pup's velvety asshole. Watching Mammoth twist, grunt, and even cry out himself (in a macho kind of pig-grunt way), Monster felt sympathy for the recipient of his pool-cue dick: Hate to have that thing whipped and jerking on top of me, he thought.

Then, when Mammoth was done with his seizure, he said, "Fuck, Fuck, FUCK! Whew!" Panting like a bike on cheap gas that simply refused to die. "OK, asshole. Your turn."

Monster didn't say a word. He just kissed Pup on the forehead (feeling of wire bristles and lips surprisingly soft) and went over to his bike. When he walked back into the hard light spilling from the track he was carrying a pint of oil and sporting an unreadable expression.

"Fucker ain't yours yet, man," Mammoth said, hitching up his belt and laughing, low and mean, "and I don't think she needs any oil."

"Not for the fucking bike, asshole," Monster said, unbuckling his pants and dropping them to the asphalt.

If Mammoth's cock was a pool cue, then Monster's was...what? Big? Damned sure it was fucking big. I mean, think about it, do you think a mean-ass motherfucker with the handle of Monster would have an ordinary cock? No fucking way—he would have a monster cock, right? A weird cock, a twisted, patched-up, piebald, bent, swollen thing—that's what would be hanging between Monster's legs, right?

Damned right: one ball bigger than the other (marble next to bowling ball), circumcised head swollen and lopsided like it had been patched by some unlucky loser in a crap game (so the rumors said), a corkscrewed shaft like maybe he'd been hard up and wasted and tried to fuck the transmission of a hog (rumor said), long puckered scar from halfway to the base of his groin like Monster's cock had been stuck in some asshole or cunt and had to have been bled, maybe, to make it small enough to get it out (rumor again).

Of course Monster had a fucking scary cock. What else would you think?

And it was hard and throbbing.

Maybe something small and maybe even sweet took over Mammoth at that point, cause he took Pup's head in his hands and turned him so he couldn't look back and see that warped length of steel-hard pork that was about to take a trip up his ass. Maybe Mammoth had something like a burst of conscience, and maybe he was worried about what Pup might do if he saw Monster's cock.

Just maybe—'cause he knelt down and whispered in Pup's ear: "Whatever you thought it would be...it's worse."

Pup whimpered.

Pup whimpered even more after Monster popped the oil like a Bud and pooped its thick gold onto his cock and positioned himself so that he was right up against Pup's throbbing and quaking asshole.

Then in.

Pup made a noise. No, not like you'd think. Nothing to war

against the racetrack nearby and win, nothing hard and shrill and painful to hear. Pup made a noise, for sure—a simple, little kind of noise.

A good kind of noise: part groan, part grunt, part moan, part sigh. It slipped out of his lips because the slow, pleasant, progression of Monster's twisted and fat cock into Pup's asshole was done gentle and smooth, lubed with 10-40 and a glacial patience.

Pup started to buck a bit as that good noise seeped out of him, trying to force the fuck that Monster didn't seem willing to do by forcing himself back against him and then pulling away. Between them, the sound of their fucking was a wet slurping, a sucking chest wound kind of noise.

Mammoth was laughing and rocking back and forth: "Come on, you fucker, let's hear it!"

Monster smiled wide and sharp, gave Pup a hard slap against his pale, hard ass, and started to return the buck—slapping his iron thighs against Pup with a steady and building rhythm. As he did, as he humped against Pup's asshole, he started to leak out a good series of grunts too—a kind of cycling engine noise like a motor perfectly tuned and then slowly revved up to speed.

On the receiving end, Pup too started his own revving grunts as he bucked and slammed back and forth against Monster's escalating thrusts of his huge, misshapen cock. Slap, slap, SLAP!

Suddenly, Pup dropped down to the asphalt so his face was panting and heaving into the hard black surface and his ass was high in the air. Behind him, Monster could feel one of Pup's hands fumble with Monster's tight and aching balls and then vanish to, Monster guessed, stroke his own aching cock.

"I can't fucking hear you!" screamed Mammoth, rocking back and forth and laughing, laughing, laughing...

Pup screamed, then, low and growling like he'd reached down through his own cock and pulled gritty, brilliant come out of himself. He jerked like Mammoth, but a Mammoth impaled on a hot rod of corkscrewed meat: He flailed and thumped the hard road with his free hand and drooled a warm pool of spit onto the black surface.

Behind him, Monster echoed and amplified: He bellowed like a great fucking beast with his cock caught in some kind of wild suction trap. He howled like a wolf getting one bitching fucking blow job, like a lion getting it from an elephant.

Then he pulled himself out with a slurping pop, stood up with a sudden stagger, and wiped his huge brow with a denim sleeve.

Mammoth was grinning and laughing and smiling and said, "Well, motherfucker, that was damned fucking quiet. Very fucking quiet. Hope you don't plan on riding it out of here."

"Nope, didn't plan on it at all," Monster said, after hitching his belt and helping a grinning and laughing and smiling Pup to his wobbling feet. "Not at all," he added, putting a knurled hand on Pup's shoulder.

The bike, of course, went to Mammoth...and Pup? Pup went with Monster, of course.

Echoes

This guy had blond hair. Red's had been black as ink: a late night mop of unkempt curls. Same with the mustache—Red's had been a silent film villain's handlebar that, if he was going out tricking, he might or might not actually twirl into ridiculous spirals. So like Red, so very like him: head a blenderized mess, mustache prissily maintained.

The guy Chev had on his living room sofa now, though, had a perfectly maintained surfer coif. Looking at this guy, you could tell he spent way too long in front of the mirror, spraying down his perfect honey-blond locks minute after minute, making everyone late.

Red used to say, "You don't kiss with your hair. You kiss with your mustache."

This other guy, Chev wished he could remember his name, said, "Gotta bait the hook with something," when Chev said he liked his hair.

Red had liked to fuck to Japanese drums and the *1812 Overture*. This guy, this mystery of Friday night tricking, had been dancing to Frankie Goes to Hollywood and fuckin' ABBA like he'd been stricken with queer palsy: jerking and bouncing to his deep, spiritual connection to disco.

Still, Chev had to maintain, running his long, thin fingers over the blond god's chest, he really knows how to kiss.

Red had been a tough trick. Chev had pursued and hunted and chased the man till he gave up that night after Alex's birthday party. This guy (name? name?) had been too easy: An early Friday drop by the Big Ear, a tequila sunrise for strength, an ogle at the guy jerking to Go West, small talk, small talk, small talk, "I live up the block," then the couch and finding out the guy was pretty good at kissing.

Red had been good at kissing too. He'd had what he liked to call a "learned tongue, professorial lips, and a doctored mouth."

Red had liked to test your lips when he kissed: gentle little touches and scrapes with that smooth mustache, feeling your lips for softness and that subtle hint of opening. Red hadn't been a wet lamprey fastening to your mouth with suction and gallons of cold spit. He had been a strong and supple kisser, with a strong, darting tongue that was just where you wanted it. He'd had a very unique range of acrobatics with his tongue: touching tip to tip, following with tongue tantra every move you made until you were your tongue, dancing tip to tip with his. He'd liked to follow that narrow groove in your tongue as he kissed, feeling its texture and smoothness (or so he said). Chev had been with lots of guys. Bad. Good. Indifferent. Forgettable. Memorable. Only one, though, that kissed exactly like Red—and that was Red himself.

Except, Chev suddenly realized with cold, clammy shock, for this blond, empty-headed surfer clone on his sofa.

In the woods up near Mount Tam, hidden in a corner no one

visited—beneath a stunted mesquite bush, marked by nothing but a particular bluish stone, after six months Red's body was as cold as the high mountain.

The man on Chev's couch kissed exactly like Red—who was dead, from a single bullet, and buried.

Headaches can come on suddenly, he explained, shaking and stroking the guy's strong leg. Blinding migraines. Sudden pain for which the cure was a couple of extra-strength meds and sleeping in the dark. Sorry, sorry, sorry.

When the blond left with maybe a slight irritation at having wasted an hour of precious Friday night tricking time, Chev didn't take anything except a hefty shot of Black Death vodka.

Red wasn't anywhere around anymore. His books were sold or given to friends. He hadn't come with any furniture, and what few clothes he had brought ended up at Community Thrift.

Looking around his apartment, Chev couldn't see Red at all. There was nothing to show that they had lived together for six months, had fucked and kissed and talked long into the night. There was nothing to show the eventual friction, the fights, and the strange tension that had come between them. The gun had been Red's as well, a heavy revolver, probably an antique, that he had said was for protection. Chev had dropped it into the Bay on the way back from burying Red's body.

Everything of Red was gone. Not a trace.

No. Everything of Red should have been gone.

His name was Raul. And he was quite a Raul—a beautiful son of the Aztecs with a strong nose, high forehead, and skin the color of stained wood. Strong, too. Chev had been talking and sipping black Russians with Jack and Alex when Raul had been introduced as an ex of an ex. "Worth sleeping with that bastard just to get an intro to this beautiful man," Alex said, ruffling Raul's thick black locks.

He and Chev hit it off, and soon they were making the two-story trek up to Chev's flat. Raul had a few more in him, and was frisky and clutching. As Chev fumbled with his front door lock, the giant Hispanic had grabbed him around the waist and lifted him right off his feet.

Red had never lifted him like that.

Raul must have studied with Houdini. Not seeming to mind that Chev wasn't in the mood to kiss, he had Chev's belt and jeans down in seconds. Never, never, never one to protest a boy's enthusiasm, Chev just smiled as he watched Raul's excited eyes dance over his strong legs, furry crotch, and straining cock—eager for Raul.

Raul got right down to it.

And Chev screamed.

Their first time was right after Alex's birthday party. More than slightly drunk, they had stumbled back to Chev's place—mutually agreeing, silently, that they were going to go fuck.

Oh, they did all right. They did indeed. Once inside Chev's place, they fell into a hot clench. Hot mouth to hot mouth, bodies strong against each other. No prelude: just tongues dancing the fandango in each other's mouth, hands on very hard cocks beneath Chev's jeans and Red's cotton drawstrings.

Red had been a big guy, a smart guy; like some kind of strange hybrid of an 18th-century professor of philosophy and a lumberjack. That first night, after a long and luscious clench in the hall, Red had simply picked up the slight Chev, threw him neatly over his shoulder in a fireman's carry, and bumped around Chev's apartment till Chev finally stopped laughing and said, "Second door on the left."

Throwing him down—Chev instantly glad he hadn't purchased that futon he had been eyeing when he first moved in—Red made quick work of his jeans. Chev remembered it like it had just happened: Red yanking off his pants, tearing down his boxers and whistling as he eyed Chev's long, strong cock pointing just about straight up. Chev remembered Red's eyes as he measured Chev's cock: taking it all in, measuring and panting as he thought about...well, taking it all in. Chev remembered clearly, cleanly, how Red had gotten down on the small bed and kissed Chev's cock head, tasting the tiny glimmering spot of precome that had slowly formed there. "Just the thing. I'm feeling a mite peckish," Red had said, licking from the base of Chev's balls to his bobbing, throbbing head.

He remembered it too well. Raul, six months later, had said exactly the same thing, and had licked and tried to suck him—exactly, precisely, identically, the same.

But there was a difference. Maybe it took a little time for whatever Red was now to get through completely. Maybe the soil he was buried in had some special quality. Whatever the cause, as Raul got down to it, the sensations, the techniques, the performance was all dearly departed, dead, Red. It was Red sucking on Chev's cock—with all of his little tricks of tongue and lips and teeth and mouth. But, but, but something added. Red, after all, was dead and buried, rotting on Mount Tamalpais. So it was: Red was sucking on Chev's cock, a Red eaten by insects, covered in mold, bursting with putrefaction and disintegration. Raul's mouth wasn't just an echo—Raul's was the mouth of a man dead for many months.

Insects and their children squirmed around Chev's cock. A

tooth, loosened by decay, rattled and abraded against his shaft. The tissues of Raul's tongue seemed to stretch and tear and fall, loose and much too wet around his balls.

Till Chev screamed and he stopped.

Alex was an art nut. His place was little larger than Chev's, but it was so crammed with the graying, 50-plus, ex-architect's collection of sculptures, paintings, mobiles, books, and photographs that it seemed like a museum's closet.

Chev sipped Earl Grey, feeling the warmth of the Picasso mug through his cold and shivering hands.

He imagined Alex saying it just before he actually said it: "You've been under a lot of stress lately. That could be it."

Chev nodded, staring down at his warping reflection in his hot tea. "I don't want him back, Alex." He tried to keep the growing panic out of his voice, hoping dear, sweet Alex would just take it for sadness.

"There's probably a part of you that does. But you made your decision, didn't you? It just has to settle a bit, that's all."

"It's too real."

"It was a very hard decision, wasn't it? Give yourself some credit for how hard it was, Chev."

Alex and Chev's relationship had been a good one, but not all that memorable. Chev liked fire in his men—Alex was more like warm smoke. While a very good and very kind man, Alex seemed to be always somewhere else. Even in bed there was a part of Alex that always seemed to be in the next room listening to '20s jazz, looking at Postimpressionists, or feeling up a Moore sculpture. Still, Alex was kind and caring and supportive—though from across the room.

Harder than I hope you'll ever know, Alex. The body was heavy and I had to dig down very deep.

Alex knew a lot about what had gone on between Red and Chev, but not all of it. He knew about that night after his birthday party—how Big Red seemed to be just the thing for long and lanky Chev. He knew about the heat, the passion. He knew about the looks they used to give each other and how those looks changed after a point. Alex had helped Chev try to get in touch with what was going on between Red and him, and had even let Chev bunk on his couch when things got too much for him.

But Alex didn't know about that night. The gun. The mountain. He thought that Red had just left.

"He asked you and you couldn't do it," Alex said, sitting next to Chev on the sofa and putting a slightly wrinkled hand on Chev's shaking knee. "It wasn't what you wanted, but you still loved him, right? Think of it this way: if he really loved you he would still be here."

He does love me. He still is here.

"It's natural," Alex said, stroking his leg. "You're having second thoughts. Part of you wants him back and part of you is frightened of having him back—so part of him is back."

From Mount Tam and soft soil. "But I don't want him back, Alex."

"Sorry." Alex sipped his own tea. "I wish I could make it better. You know, sometimes you just have to go through it to come out the other side. You should just try and let go of the fear, the pain. Tolerate it so you'll know that he's not here, not with you, that he's really gone."

Chev could only nod.

"Remember, I'm here for you"

"I know that, Alex." *So is Red.*

Red hadn't really been a racist; he simply wasn't turned on by black men. It was something they used to laugh over—back when they could laugh together—cruising the crowds coming and going from the Castro: "He's for you," Red would say when a gorgeous black man walked by.

His name was John. He seemed a nice enough guy.

John had been folding sheets down at the Spindizzie Laundromat. Even if Chev wasn't looking for something to take his mind off Red, he probably still would have approached John; tall and thin, but with a broad chest and a face composed of soft features pressed on a hard skull. He didn't look like a baby; more like someone without much of life stamped on him.

He was as black as powdered chocolate. Chev hoped, strongly, that he really, truly wasn't Red's type.

John may not have been experienced, but he was certainly enthusiastic. The thin hook Chev laid for him was that Chev had a rare copy of a Billie Holiday album (he didn't, but Alex did). The hook might have been thin, but John tagged right along.

Inside Chev's little place, things got tense. Between John's shyness and Chev's mounting panic over what might happen, all they did for almost an hour was hunt for the mythical record. Finally, after splitting a spit-soaked roach over their failure to locate Ms. Holiday's record, they found themselves dry-humping in the kitchen. There was something powerful about the shy black man, something that, for a moment, was like a wave crashing into and through Chev: He felt John's excitement like a kind of surge in himself and, despite a tiny voice screaming panic in his ear, soon Chev's cock was screaming for the touch of a hand, a mouth, an asshole—anything!

They stumbled into the bedroom, John whispering a mantra of "beautiful, beautiful, beautiful..." as Chev slipped off his shirt, yanked off his shoes, and dropped his pants.

As John leapt for his cock, Chev pushed him carefully away. "Let me," he said, trying to cling to some kind of control. He had a plan—or hoped he would after John pulled down his pure white boxers and showed off his own lovely, straining cock—no more Mr. Passive. He had been that with Red, he had always been on the receiving end of everything: his ridiculous rules, his demands on his precious time, everything. Maybe if he could turn the other way...break the pattern...escape.

Gently, he pushed John back on the bed and set to work on his cock. John tasted of salty precome, with a gentle background of healthy sweat and a hint of old soap in his coarse, black, curly pubic hairs. His cock was large and had a beautiful (Chev couldn't help saying it, making John smile) shape to it—a gentle tapering to a smooth, almost pointed, uncircumcised head.

Chev kissed it, licked its length, tasted the salt again.

Then he put John's cock in his mouth.

It wasn't John's cock anymore

In a flash of heated seconds (ringing of the near-madness of total panic), Chev wasn't tasting thick black skin and salty sweat. He was tasting rot, the foul bitterness of decomposition, and the sickly sweet smell of corruption. He was sucking on a bloated, dirt-choked worm of a cock, a wrinkled finger oozing puss and insect larva.

He didn't scream. He almost made it to the toilet before throwing up on the chilled tile floors.

At least John was nice. He soothed and calmed the quaking and crying Chev till almost dawn—then he had to go to work.

This time the tea tasted like blood. That, or maybe he had bit his mouth or tongue the night before.

Morning. John was a fading memory, and Alex actually looked…ruffled. He made Chev tea and toast with a kind of waking somnambulism that Chev had never seen before. But then he'd never gotten the gray-haired ex-architect up at 6 in the morning before.

"How are you doing?" Alex said, sitting next to him, leaning against him.

"Better." Normally Chev didn't like to be reminded of the more physical past of their relationship. Normally he liked to consider Alex "just a friend." Normally he felt a good portion of guilt and self-hatred over his coolness toward his old ex-lover. But that morning, Alex was something warm, caring, and familiar.

"You need help," Alex said, stifling a yawn and sipping his tea.

"No shit," Chev said, full of grim uselessness and sarcasm.

"You know he's gone."

"Also, no shit." *Can't get more gone than a bullet.*

"Did you see him recently? Maybe that's it?"

Chev shook his head. "He's long gone."

"Do you feel guilty about him leaving?"

I killed him, Alex. I shot him. I put his body in my car and drove him up to the mountains and buried him. "I guess so."

"You have to get over it."

"Don't you think I want to?"

Alex sighed, put his cup down on the floor and put his head on Chev's shoulder. The older man's breath was a warm patch on Chev's chest. "I think you'd like to. I don't know if you can." Absently, Alex started to play with the buttons on Chev's shirt.

It had always been that way between them—the cruel kind of game that ex-lovers play when they need each other too much but have grown apart. Alex pursued and Chev ignored. This time

Chev was simply too tired, too scared. Alex was there, as Alex had been before, would be again and again, to take care of him and try to make things right. This time Chev might just let him.

Chev didn't protest as Alex managed to get his shirt buttons undone. It was like coming home. It was like being a teenager again and necking on the rec room couch.

"What more do you want?" Red had said when they had shared a couch too. "Aren't I enough for you?"

"If this upsets you," Alex was saying, as he undid the last button, "please, just say no."

Lost in the familiarity and the comfort of Alex, Chev did nothing but nod softly, letting his old friend Alex rub his smooth hands up and down Chev's faintly haired chest and over his hardening nipples.

"He's gone, Chev. You just have to face that."

"Your home is here with me now," Red said with simple words and soft tones. "Don't you want me to be here with you? I thought we might make a home together. Wouldn't you like that?"

"You made your decision. You didn't want him around anymore." Alex deftly undid Chev's belt and slipped his soft cotton pants to the floor. Chev's BVDs were tented with his hard cock— hard from the comfort in Alex's words.

"You don't own me," Chev had said, gripped with panic, confused and feeling trapped, seeing nothing but Red, and ready to chew off his own foot to escape. But he had also wanted no one but Red. But he had also been scared of not being free, of being trapped with the man. No, with any man.

"Relax and just be here with me, now," Alex said, pulling Chev's underwear down and softly stroking his hard, smooth cock.

"I don't want to own you. I love you. I want to be with you— forever if I could," Red had said.

"It's just me now. Just old Alex. You know I wouldn't hurt you, Chev." Alex's soft lips bathed his cock in satin skin. Alex's mouth was wet and hot—like a tiny sauna over his straining cock. It felt good. It felt like home. Safe.

"I want to be with you. Why is that so scary? Why are you so angry because I love you? Damn it, Chev, I want to be with you. I want to live with you, play with you, and grow old with you. Why are you so scared?"

Red used to do exactly the same thing. The same hot mouth. The same bath of steaming saliva and—there—the same scrapes of teeth across Chev's cock head.

The gun had been heavy in Chev's hand, so solid and firm—not like his thoughts, stabbing at his mind and his body. His gut had ached, his legs had felt cramped. He wanted, he wanted, he wanted—he wanted Red, he wanted out, he wanted to be in love with him always, he wanted to be free. He wanted to stop hurting. He wanted to stop being so panicked and confused.

The one thing he didn't want to do was pull the trigger.

"You have to live with what happened," Alex said, stopping his cock sucking to stare up at Chev with kind eyes. "You didn't want to settle down. He did. He left. You stayed. It's your decision and you have to accept it."

The gun was a small caliber. The shot was perfect. It was late at night and the street was quiet. He was lucky. Down the stairs and into his battered old car and up into the hills. He told anyone who asked that they had fought and Red had left.

Alex licked and sucked his cock again. Tasting the saltiness of his excitement and the strength of him. Red had done exactly the same thing...

"He's gone, Chev. Be here, with me."

...exactly. But then it wasn't exactly the same. It was still Red working his cock, but it was Red under the dirt on top of the mountain. Worms. Dirt. Dust and bones. The same nips and washes of Red's tongue. The same caresses with his cheeks and the gentle pressure of the back of his throat on the head of Chev's cock. Corroding flesh peeling and breaking over his softening cock, maggots wriggling and nibbling at his thin skin, the slick liquid of pus washing down and over him.

Crying and screaming, Chev reached down and pushed and pulled at the sensations, at the unceasing cock sucking of dead and rotting Red.

Somewhere Alex was saying, "Just relax. It's for your own good."

Chev panicked and pushed and heaved and bucked and tried to get Alex to stop. Chev's scream burned his chest and ripped his throat apart. His panic was hot metal in his arms and his legs. His hands were flying everywhere, trying to get Alex to stop.

Then Alex did stop. Breathing too. He rolled heavy and empty onto the floor. His eyes were still and quiet. His chest didn't move. His lips were slack and faintly gray.

Chev could still feel his hands around Alex's throat, trying to push Red away—trying to push the all-encompassing love of Red away.

Robot, Chev got up, adjusted himself, and walked out the door.

Luckily, he had enough in his bank account for a ticket. Luckily, he had his passport up-to-date. Luckily, Chev knew, good picture framers could find work almost anywhere.

Chev lost himself in his panic and the run. In his more lucid moments—half asleep on the transpacific plane, waiting to pass through customs, watching strange television in his first hotel—he allowed himself to actually think. But when his thoughts turned to Alex slowly cooling on the floor, or the feeling of Red, he tried not to do it anymore. Just doing what I've always done, he actually thought once—just once—I'm running away from it all.

Back home, he knew, things would go on without him. Like he had never really happened. A few rough spots, maybe—like his disappearance, like Alex's death—but he knew it would be like nothing had ever happened before too long. The police never cared. They would chalk it up to what it was: a strangulation accident. Sure, some of his friends would think of him with suspicion or hate. But then others would get the same look. People left suddenly all the time: Thailand, France, New York, and yes, even Australia. Alex was sweet, lovable, Alex—warm and reassuring, kind and gentle, popular and giving. You can't interrogate or blame everyone who'd ever sat on Alex's couch and sipped tea, or anyone who traveled quickly, impulsively.

It was many months before Chev went to a club. First he found work in a place all too similar to his old job. Then he found a room, and then a small apartment. It was many months before he was comfortable going outside and feeling anything like free. Many months before he could be touched without looking for something of dead and decaying Red in it.

Finally, he did it. Finally, he got drunk enough to get picked up by a burly guy named Nick. Nick seemed bound and determined to prove that Aussies could give and get as good as someone from the mecca of San Francisco. Chev actually laughed at his humor and his sparkling smile. He felt light as Nick hauled Chev off to his tiny room, poured a whole tin of Fosters down him, and set to work on what he called "the Australian Crawl"— his one-of-a-kind cock and balls treat.

For a minute, Chev was there in the room with the bawdy Australian. He was there laughing and feeling good again after so much death and the echoes of same. He was free and easy and, while things were hazy with the passing of Alex, he knew that it would all be OK. The Australian was fun, and his cock sucking was nothing, nothing, nothing like Red. Not at all.

The sensations of Nick's one-of-a-kind cock suck filtered through Chev: the tongue work, the teeth touches, the washes of tongue. Nothing like Red.

But perfectly, exactly, like poor, dead, Alex.

Blue Boy

"Sure you won't?" Mr. Oleander said, fondling the fine, supple neck of a sweet young thing. A girl, delicate and blue. As a boss, Oleander was a lethargic mountain—slow but unstoppable in his decisions. Luckily for the firm of Oleander, Destar and West—designers of fine imitation antiques—his mountain was formed by tried-and-true decisions.

Prosper shook his head: a slow, tired movement of boredom. Girls didn't interest him. In fact...

Oleander traced the contours of the young girl's lovely neck and shoulders. Even Prosper, who had seen his share of lovely necks, had to watch—hypnotized by the subtle geometry of her throat and the beginning slope of chest.

She wore a perfect lithograph dress, slightly bluer than the blue of her skin. An ideal Alice, a snapshot Dorothy, an identical Wendy. Crinoline, lace, and tiny cream-colored shoes. Her sunset-glowing hair was highlighted by a pink silk bow.

"I know she's not exactly your type, but...you positive?" Oleander asked. He had the girl balanced perfectly on his fat knee. The girl and Oleander—he a rolling surge of dark, strong meat, pressed into a fine Osaka suit—were a picture. The picture wouldn't have been pretty if the girl hadn't been such a lovely shade of blue.

Prosper had enjoyed his share of blues in his quite young life. Not Alices, Dorothies, or Wendies, but Hucks, Rudolphs, and Troys beyond count. A great many. A great many—far above the National Average. Still, this one, this one girl, was *such* a lovely shade. Despite the lack of interest in her sex, Prosper still had to watch, if just for her magnificent color: early dawn, shallow ocean, a robin's egg.

Lovely, lovely blue.

With refinement and dexterity, Oleander reached out a fat, walnut-colored hand. Prosper knew from 20 years of Hucks, Rudolphs, and Troys that she wouldn't bat an eyebrow. Letting a lemonade and peppermint smile play around her porcelain features, she absently kicked her little legs—balancing on Oleander's massive knee as he moved. She didn't even flinch when Oleander picked up the finely crafted wooden box from his desk.

Simple in its beauty. Teak. Oleander skillfully opened it with one hand, a gesture rehearsed by endless repetition. In another age, it would have been lighting a cigarette, producing identification, or checking a pocket watch.

Oleander took the young girl's head and tilted it back. Animated with a girl-like glow, she complied. Then he kissed her fine throat, just a grazing of his thick lips along the cerulean column of her neck.

"Don't know what you're missing," he said.

Again, Prosper shook his head. He knew exactly what he was missing. Exactly; he knew what had been in the box and what was now in his boss's hand, knew the antique straight razor's weight, contours, and even its oily smell. Prosper knew the way it fell into the skin, the way the steaming blue blood poured out and onto the hand that held it. He also knew the feel of rope, the greasy mass of a pistol, the heft of a candlestick, and much, much more.

He knew the smell after: copper and salt. Knew it all very well.

Oleander expertly slit the girl's fine blue throat. The razor slid into her skin, two inches at least. A very fine knife. A good razor. The kind of quality one would correctly expect for the leading partner of Oleander, Destar, and West. For a beat of his heart, Prosper was caught up in the act of Oleander slicing the girl open—but it was a catch of reminiscence rather than attraction.

Seen one, seen a thousand.

The girl's blood poured out of her, running down the razor and over Oleander's hand. The leading partner had a connoisseur's touch: As the blood ran, he tipped his razor just-so and pale blue blood, even paler than the girl's skin, flowed onto the same-colored carpeting.

None of the blood fell on Oleander's lovely suit. Instead, it soaked her dress, all but making it vanish with the flow—fainter blue against fainter blue.

As the girl died, Oleander put his lips to her cheek, kissing her softly as she drained of fluid, potential, future, and resale value.

Dead, Oleander tipped her from his lap with a practiced movement, gripping her neck from behind and pushing her slight body away from him until she dangled like a puppet at the end of his huge arm. Being careful to avoid the quickly evaporating pool of azure blood at his feet, Oleander took the small corpse to a carefully unfurnished corner of his vast office and dropped her with a tumble of flaccid limbs.

Dabbing at his immaculate hands with a lovely lace handkerchief, Oleander sat down again and smiled—a contented play of dazzling eyes and widely grinning lips. "Much better. Does wonders for the blood pressure, you know."

Prosper nodded, smiling back but feeling nothing. Nothing at all.

"Now," Oleander said, knitting his large fingers together over his belly and fixing Prosper with calm eyes, "about the redesign of those Jivaro skinning knives...."

Somewhere—he was unsure of where, exactly—Prosper had heard that certain occupations were manufactured en masse. Street cleaners, clerks, clowns, prostitutes, ticket collectors, repair people: streaming out of the huge upstate factories.

The newspaper vendor in the lobby, for instance, was different from the one when Prosper entered that morning. Prosper remembered the vendor's slightly lopsided head, his slight facial twitch. (Abnormalities both subtle and gross were a common design theme: What better to exorcise the hate and fear of the unusual than on disposable, easily replaceable Blues?) Prosper remembered his irritating voice and his scowling eyes too. Someone must have blown out his brains, stabbed him, slit his throat, crushed his skull or killed him in any one of a thousand other ways earlier in the day. Now his stall was clean, immaculate—without even the telltale sign of another Blue mopping up the former vendor's cerulean blood.

Prosper bought his evening paper without even a thought for the old proprietor except to notice he was no longer there. After all, he'd only been there since last night. Someone had stuck a sawed-off shotgun into the belly of his predecessor the afternoon before. Prosper remembered it clearly, mainly because he'd had to walk through a pool of his quickly evaporating blood to buy a nicotine stick.

Outside, Prosper let the city wash over him, the usual sights and sounds of his way home blurring into an endlessly repeating kaleidoscope of store-fronts, smiling commuters, flickering advertisements, and diligently working street cleaners, clerks, clowns, prostitutes, ticket collectors, and repair people, all replaced as soon as someone killed them.

The frustration was a wire in Prosper. As he usually did, had done, for almost three months now, he thought about killing. He thought about it as he entered the subway, looking at the pleasant-faced girl in the ticket booth, at her sparkling smile and firework eyes. He thought about taking her head in his hands and banging it, again and again, against the pink-tiled wall of the subway platform. He knew exactly how it would feel: the echoing vibration of each smack of her against the wall. The way her head would shake in his hands, how the feel of it, the solidity of it, would change as her skull cracked and then changed shape with each fevered impact. He knew exactly how the sound would change as the back of her head flattened, then seeped blood— blue, quick-evaporating blood.

He knew, after a point, as he slammed her harder and harder against the tiles, that her blood would seep and then splatter. He knew there was that special, magical moment when her skull would just simply collapse from his passionate, diligent pounding, how in one instant he'd go from holding an intact head to holding a globe of broken plates, mushy tissue and brains.

Done one, done a thousand. Prosper passed her his ticket and she let him onto the platform.

He knew he should still be thinking about work, mulling over the nuances of Mr. Oleander's timbre and choice of words, but all he could seem to summon was an overwhelming sadness and a deep, all-but-hidden whipcord of painful frustration.

Again, he debated killing. There were several Blues on the platform: an old-looking couple scowling at all the young and energetic, an arrogant buck in a leather jacket, a tiny boy in a (naturally) blue sailor suit who cried hysterically and annoyingly, a very pleasant-looking young man in a white shirt and tight jeans.

Looking at the latter, he ran a quick fantasy though his mind—with the perfect detail that came from many, many (too many) real experiences. The platform wasn't crowded, more than enough room for a quick one. The scene rolled through his mind in perfect clarity: walk up to his bountiful Blue form; a quick slap to knock him off balance; a tear at his shirt to view the geometry of his chest; a shove to bring him to his knees; unzip and jam a too-hard cock in his mouth; feel him swallow and gulp it down through artificial moans and complaints; maybe fuck him, turn him around, yank down those tight jeans and stuff a cock into the warm, expertly designed asshole; and then do it—a knife, a gun, whatever—shooting white come into a steaming bath of blue blood.

Done one.... Why do one more?

The train pulled into the station, sliding in with no noise save for the screams and wet sounds of the little boy's body. Prosper blinked, joining the queue to enter, suddenly realizing he had missed the boy being tossed onto the tracks. Distracted.

In the train, he took his usual seat. Across from him, a pair of Blue workmen in stained and dirty coveralls bagged the corpse of an old lady, cleaning the wall and seat where she had been sitting. The map of brilliantly colored routes was temporarily obscured by her rapidly vanishing blood. With the absentness of trying to remember the next line of a popular song or what he'd had for breakfast the day before, Prosper tried to figure the murder weapon. He had all but decided on a *katana* because of the very clean way her head had been separated from her body and the way her blood had fanned onto the route map, but then he noticed the tall, thin black man sitting two seats back—and the Maori ceremonial knife in his lap (still a faint blue). One of Oleander, Destar, and West's own products. A very successful line.

Prosper remembered his therapist. He'd selected Gordon more or less on a whim after visiting three or four of his profession. Gordon had an easy voice, a sleepy style that went completely against the hysteria that Prosper felt day after day. The calm demeanor made it easier to talk to the man, to have a still pool to drop his sharp, rattling angers and frustrations into for an hour.

"Set a goal, Josh. Make it simple. No big plans, no immediate reward. The strangle job is a good one, but you still think about it too much. Just do it. Set a time limit—tomorrow at lunch or the first thing in the morning. Carry a knife if it'll make you feel better. Be spontaneous rather than plotting. When you feel like it, just do it. You take the subway, right? Push one onto the tracks. The more you wait, the more frustrated you'll be. You'll be surprised at how much better you'll feel."

Westerberg: The neighborhood smelled of dusk, the slow-moving Mongusti river, and bad Chinese food. Once again, walking home, Prosper thought about killing. Even though the Gung Ho had been closed since someone had machine-gunned the entire blue staff one night—and the owner hadn't gotten around to replacing them or reopening the place—the neighborhood, by law, had its proportion. A boy in plus-fours and suspenders bounced a ball on one corner. A panhandler, all drug palsy, missing teeth, and aggressive palm, moved through the commuting crowd. A Playmate of the Moment lounged against one of the Gung Ho's boarded-up windows, spandex skirt hiked high to show a lack of panties as she scowled her disdain. The only one that caught Prosper's direct attention was a cop, who watched commuters leave the station through mirrored sunglasses and uttered an abusive "Fucking homo queer" as Prosper strolled past.

Prosper thought about killing him. The cop would be slow, since he was a blue: easy to push him over, fumble his revolver out of his holster (against his surprisingly feeble protests), click the hammer back, and fire three or four rounds into his helmeted head. Prosper guessed that he would scream and plead and soil his immaculate uniform with blue piss. And Prosper knew, fucking knew, his head would explode with the first round, face blooming forward but confined by the helmet.

Prosper shook his head sadly and entered his building. He was surprised, pleasantly, to find the lobby and elevator free of the evidence of murder. It lifted his spirits to have a clean slate for once. He felt his muscles relax against their gripping tightness of frustration. *Yeah, maybe,* he thought. *Maybe tonight. A fresh start—something unique.*

He started to think about his kitchen, his sample case of half a dozen finely crafted weapons. Hadn't done a circular saw in a while, hadn't done a spear since two years ago at the Mass Murder Street Fair. Shotguns were fun too, and he had the one, unused, that his father had given him for his birthday two years ago.

But it vanished, evaporating as everything seemed to do, in just a few moments. He put his key in his door and went in.

"The first developments in Blue technology," went the announcer from his blaring television, "were, of course, in the field of nanomolecular engineering, leading to the first prototype fetus in 2015—"

The channel flipped as he hung his coat. "Cerulean Industries today announced a new line of Blues dedicated to less-represented ethnic types. As part of the Stereotype series, Cerulean plans a modification of the current Gook, Kike and Nig—" The announcer was, as always, new: Prosper caught sight of her as he walked in, noting the standard saccharine smile and glittering eyes. He doubted he'd tune in to watch the audience poll of how to kill her at the end of the broadcast.

"Oh," said Troy from the couch, taking his eyes off the flickering set long enough to nail Prosper with arrogant boredom, "you're home." The television flipped, again and again, until it finally settled on a flashy commercial for a new line of Sex/Death Blues called "Come Hither." The television glow painted Troy's normally dark blue skin almost purple.

Prosper went into the kitchen and poured himself two fingers of scotch, kicking back the flames and closing his eyes. From the living room, Troy said, "So, shit-head, are you gonna kill me tonight or what?"

Prosper knocked back another drink.

"So how was work, dear?"

The liquor burned, a flaming trail from the back of his throat to the unknown depths of his stomach. The sensation felt good—feeling anything felt good.

Prosper shrugged, breathing heavy over the sink. He didn't see, didn't care, if Troy saw the gesture.

"Had a very exciting day, myself. Saw a *Life Without Hope* I hadn't seen before."

"Happy for you," Prosper said, panting into the sink, fighting the liquor that was struggling back up. Troy had been an indulgence. Oleander, Destar, and West paid well enough that he could easily afford someone every few days or so. He'd had Troy for three months. An eternity for a Blue.

"Almost enough to get out of fucking bed for."

His breath was acid, breathing burned his sinuses. The pain

was real and sharp. He panted until the room started to tilt, enjoying the sensation. Troy had originally been part of some-thing...elaborate. But it had never materialized. Troy had become furniture, but not as comfortable.

"You would have loved it. Tristan—you know, the illegitimate son of Vera-De and Despar Cosmo, heir to the Cosmo fortune—has this problem. A kind of intimate, manly problem. And he was having all these kinds of troubles keeping people from finding out. That is, until this one person, and, you know, I can't recall completely if he was Blue or not, just happened to speak to just the wrong person." Troy tsk-tsked, still staring, fixated, on the flickering screen. "Poor Tristan..."

The knife's handle was cold, and that surprised Prosper. Maybe from keeping it in the dark kitchen drawer. Or maybe it was just that his blood was so hot, so hammering with heat.

He took it out of the drawer—cool, cool in his hand—and walked the four steps from his kitchen to the living room. Troy turned his head, ultrasmooth as if on finely machined bearings, a movement beyond anyone save Troy's make, model. Prosper pon-dered, as he walked and raised the knife, about their mechanics. He really didn't understand the details. But you didn't need to know how a bus worked to ride on one, or how a screen worked to watch it—or turn it off.

Tension thrummed in his arm as he stabbed down. The leather of the couch drank the blade till it hit something more solid than stuffing. The impact jerked up his arm, echoing the pain of the scotch.

Troy looked at the vibrating knife, then turned back to the screen. A sound, something like a sarcastic sigh but without enough real care to properly voice it, slipped from his azure lips.

Prosper slammed his knotted fist into the side of Troy's

head. The sound of thick egg shells cracking was sharp, a voltage spark in the room. Troy's body jerked with the blow, and a deep-toned groan grumbled from his chest.

Prosper pulled the knife from the couch, hauled the Blue up by his hair, and with a blurring fury pressed the blade against his throat.

Prosper's cock was stone, iron. He ground his pelvis against the back of the couch, relishing the feeling, the humming frustration coming from the Blue.

After time had passed, glacial and tense, Troy pushed forward, sliding his neck along the blade. Prosper saw him move, felt the knife glide across his neck, smelled Troy's blood mixing with the stale room air: salt and copper adding to dust and sunlight.

Prosper pulled the knife away from Troy's straining neck, crumpled his fingers into a shaking fist, and slammed the fist into the back of Troy's head, snaking the knife out of the way as the blue fell.

"Motherfucker," panted Troy from the narrow valley between the screen and the couch, panting and rubbing the side of his head. Prosper could see that his neck was softly bleeding.

Leaving him, Prosper went back to the kitchen and put the knife away. Troy wouldn't touch it. Blues couldn't.

The thought of killing Troy churned Prosper's stomach, knotting his guts with frustrated boredom. Troy would just have to wait. Living to die, Troy was aching to. Killing him would be deadly dull; keeping him breathing, at least, was not.

Crossing the living room with heavy steps, Prosper claimed his coat and opened the door.

"If you kill anyone else I don't want to fucking hear about it," Troy said, glaring up at him with brilliant blue eyes.

Without looking back, Prosper stepped outside and slammed the door behind him.

The old stairwell echoed, carrying a heavy drumbeat tune from the machines in the basement. Prosper liked to go to the stairwell. He kept it in reserve—going there only when Things Got Very Bad. He'd been there maybe five times since his...problem first started. He wondered, feeling depression and anger rise in his chest, how many times he'd visit it again.

A dirty and all-but-abandoned stairwell, he knew, was rare, a priceless gift. Hanging on the cool metal of the railing, Prosper kicked at the crumbling stonework that had fallen on the landing from high above. He caught a vision of thin standing water over tile, rust inching up the banister, mildew like slow red ripples crawling the walls.

Go out, he told himself. Just do it. *Go out. Walk someplace, anyplace. Get a gun and do it. Don't worry about freshness, uniqueness—just break out of it. You know that's that way, you can feel it.*

Anything. Remember that young one two years ago, the one outside the museum, how you slid the knife in under his ribs and watched his pale blood trickle out? Got soaked all the way through, holding him in your lap and letting his blood leak. Remember how you held him, and rocked him as he bled early morning sky onto the sidewalk?

Or that one you surprised last fall. Remember him? Bodybuilder, all full of himself and his royal muscles. God, what a monster—all bluff and steam. Remember how you dragged him out of that bar, smashed him to the street with a barstool, then stood there on his head as he screamed and tried to reach up and knock you off? Remember your little improv dance number, until his skull gave up and you fell through a spongy turquoise brain, landing with a jolt on the cement. Laugh riot that one.

Remember the boy? Maybe, just barely, 18? Such a delightful present to yourself. A special treat, a glorious gift. All night he lasted. So skillful you were with the scalpel, the cuts. From sex to sapphire blood, from the wetness of his mouth, his ass, to the wetness of his wounds, his holes. He was so good, remember, that you just snapped his neck with the dawn—applause for a night in purest heaven?

How many glorious others, Prosper? One? Two? Three?

The splash broke him from his self-examination.

"Hello." Black leather pants: a thin coating over a finely honed body. White T-shirt over a perfect ribbed chest, nipples showing through as he moved. Streaks of blond eyebrows drawing perfect attention to pale blue eyes. A finely shaped face, a pleasant fall between full and thin. Good bones. Lips like a perfect stroke of a brush. They looked like they might taste, and feel, like silk.

"Fine night for it," he said, smiling at Prosper, bathing him in light, despite the fading sun.

"For what?" Prosper managed, still trying to climb back into the real world from his thoughts and ennui.

"Navel gazing," he said, smiling a flash of white teeth.

" 'Fraid I've been doing way too much of that of late. Hard to climb back out sometimes."

"Problem?"

"Nothing that won't get better, I guess."

He was standing close. Prosper could feel the burning between them. Prosper's eyes hummed from his delicious shape to his ideal face.

"If there's anything I can do..." He went to the railing and stared at nothing—just standing there, waiting for Prosper.

Even though it wasn't exactly his style, Prosper ran a finger up his spine, tracing the bumps of his bones with a gentle touch.

He made a soft sound and smiled back at Prosper, grinning lights.

Prosper stepped up and in, bathing his chilled, nervous self in his warmth. His cock was metal and ached with a good kind of ache. It felt good.

Prosper moved his hands around his chest, feeling his tits—flat and hard—with his palms, the tips of his fingers. Prosper hadn't felt anything like him for...ever. He was dazzling, alive with sparkling. Prosper found it hard to look at any one single thing about him—his blond hair, the lovely slope of the back of his neck. Prosper kissed the back of his neck.

He moaned, high and sweet, pushing back against Prosper's straining cock.

Hands falling to his waist, he pulled his T-shirt out of the tight pants. Giving permission, he lifted his hands above his head. The shirt came off.

Turning around, he smiled. Chest firm and cool. He had a silken belly, a gentle patch that played so well with his muscles: something gentle mixed with strength.

Prosper kissed him, tasting a faint lingering of wine, a memory of...garlic? Their tongues touched and danced a ballet of warm and wet, firm and coarse. Prosper felt them burn, ignite. Distantly, Prosper knew he was rubbing his cock through his pants, tugging at his waistband, pulling down Prosper's zipper.

The stairwell was cool, touching cold, but Prosper's cock was hot as his hands explored him. Like a fever, Prosper felt desire blast through him.

He worked at his pants. They were tight, so he backed against the railing for leverage before working them down over his strong hips, corded thighs.

He kissed Prosper again, as penetrating as a fuck, as aggressive. He turned and bent over the railing.

He was like an oven inside. A wet, tight, oven. Prosper fucked him, almost afraid that the heat of his asshole would burn his cock, would light him like a fuse and blow him away.

So good, Prosper thought; *so hot, so new.*

Then he let go, his orgasm mixing with a high point in Prosper's own moans and near-screams. Relief and the little death surged through Prosper as he managed (barely) to step back and shove his still-hard cock into his pants.

So hot, so hot. So nice and refreshing. Only one thing to make it better, perfect.

Quick and hard, Prosper knocked him off balance by kicking the back of his knee. Dropping hard, hand skipping across the rusted metal railing, he collapsed. Prosper kicked his face. The impact was hard and meaty, traveling up Prosper's leg to his cock and his smile—both very hard.

The man moaned and whimpered, clutching his mouth. He looked up at Prosper with shocked and scared blue eyes.

Prosper kicked him again, aiming for his jaw, and the stairwell echoed with the wet gong of skull on railing.

Kneeling, Prosper took his wheezing, gasping face in his hands. "So new," he said, as he slammed him back, again and again, against the metal. A fevered blur, impact after impact, gong after gong, each flowing perfectly, hotly, into the next. One. Two. Three. Four. A tempo, background rhythm. Until there wasn't enough of his head to pound.

Prosper knelt in a slowly growing pool, held thick fragments of bone and sticky blood.

"Very nice," he said, in an absent kind of voice, standing.

Brushing his hands on his pants, he was startled by how sticky they were. Looking down, he saw the mess his pants had become.

The roar came from his gut, his stomach, his balls. It tore through his lungs and up his throat. He felt the liquor boiling up. Then the impact. From behind. A flash of an azure hand and he fell, down to his knees, onto the floor, sticky with red blood.

Red.

Pain woke him. Pain and the strangeness behind his eyes. He remembered being given something, and having something taken.

Something gone: Slowly he realized which part of him was gone. The humming frustration. Exorcised. He couldn't, he realized, ever kill again—or even fight back.

Something given: He brushed a brilliant blue hand across his brilliant blue brow.

Looking down and up the alley he saw people moving to and fro at either end. Some looked his way, but most didn't even notice him. It was early; most were too busy going and coming to indulge in anything Blue.

Slowly, dancing back into the shadows, Prosper thought: *unique.* Smiling: yes, *unique.*

Matches

The dyke couple in 6C were the first to notice the gas leak, but they were in the first rushes of move-in love and lust, and simply thought it was the general ambiance of their new neighborhood. The young one, a tiny thing named Lissa, was going to mention it to the landlord, Mr. Skila, when he came for the rent, but all he ever did was nod and say, "Yes, yes, yes," in his thick (Bulgarian, Russian, Czech, Spanish, Greek?) accent and stare at her tiny tits. So she didn't.

The guy who worked at the java place around the corner was right under them, so it would have been safe to assume that he had been aware of the distinct smell of leaking natural gas—except he had lost his sense of smell in a freebasing accident (which was also why he sported his spotty and totally unattractive beard).

The apartment in front of him was probably vacant; no one could remember seeing anyone enter or leave. Rumors, at least among the tenants who spoke to each other, were that the previous occupant of 1A: (1) died, and Mr. Skila couldn't deal with getting rid of the possessions; (2) had done so much damage to the room that the lazy (Bulgarian, Russian, Czech, Spanish, Greek?) landlord couldn't be bothered fixing it up; or (3) still lived there. Fact was, most of the residents of the sad Victorian simply didn't speak to each other. The chance that yet another freak, loser, weirdo, or some such lived in the room—very quietly—was all too possible.

Above the mystery of 1A was the mystery of R. Ruge. Since R. Ruge worked late at night and slept during the day, he was rarely seen. When he was, it was on the stairs, walking up from BART, or, rarely, leaving his cave in search of greasy fast food. He didn't talk, didn't move or pause in his grinding trudge, so the other tenants saw him as a kind of clockwork; he would come slowly stomping up the stairs—bags of dripping burgers, fries, or chicken in his bloated yellow arms—filling the tiny, dark halls like a cholesterol steamroller. He was so big and unsociable that the other tenants simply stepped into the nearest doorway and let him rumble past. R. Ruge may have smelled the gas leak, but he never told anyone, let alone Mr. Skila, about it.

There were other people in the building, of course. The last number on the bashed and scarred mailbox in the lobby was 8C. But the explosion took place at 2 o'clock on a Saturday afternoon and most of them were out having lives.

The exact cause wasn't known until investigators from the San Francisco Fire Department traced the leak to Mr. Skila's workroom in the basement. No one was shocked to discover the cause of the massive explosion that killed six people, destroyed the building, and damaged several other structures in the neighborhood. Mr. Skila drank—evidenced by the bottle usually seen in the back pocket of his paint-stained jeans—and Mr. Skila smoked—evidenced by the ever-present pack of Marlboros in his shirt pocket—and Mr. Skila rarely bathed—evidenced by the garlic, stale tobacco, farts, shit, and sweat that could be smelled 200 yards away. It was easy to imagine Mr. Skila taking a break in his workroom, knocking back a good hefty swallow or two from his flask, and then lighting up a cigarette, totally unable—senses dead from the smoking and the drinking and his own reek—to tell he was taking his drink and smoke break in a room filled with gas.

R. Ruge's first name was Robert. He worked in an electronics warehouse in South City, filling little polyethylene bags with resistors, transistors, capacitors, and tiny bits of wire. He was born in Sacramento. He graduated high school, but not college. His first job was in a garage, doing lube jobs and balancing truck tires. He left home when he was 25, shortly after his first kiss: a sailor named Billy, home to visit his mother. Robert moved to the city in '69 and had a lot of fun for a few years: this bar, that bar, this guy, that guy. He avoided catching anything serious (or very serious), but he began to suffer in the looks department. Too many burgers, not enough exercise. His scores got harder and harder, and then he was having to pay, then pay more, and then pay much more. His hair was almost gone. His teeth were bad. After a point, it was easier not to try. Up until that Saturday afternoon, one of his favorite things to do was drink Budweiser, watch *American Gladiators,* and masturbate.

When the explosion roared up from Mr. Skila's workroom, Robert Ruge was going into the kitchen for another can. He wore his Saturday morning comforts: tattered old bathrobe (red with yellow stripes), old boxer shorts (once white), and the crazy-looking bunny slippers his mother had mailed to him before she died two years ago. As he stepped from the tiny living room into the even tinier kitchen, the pressure wave from the explosion smashed into the floor below, throwing him to the left, off the greasy stove and out the window. The last physical thing Robert Ruge experienced was the vibrating pain of his elbow smashing into the enamel of the stove.

R. Ruge was the second person to die that Saturday afternoon. Mr. Skila had been the first (in a flash of light). The guy who worked at the java joint was the fourth, followed by the two young dykes.

The third was the mystery in room 1A.

Death, Robert Ruge decided, wasn't half bad.

His body, at least in the last ten years or so, had been pretty much of a burden: fat, weak, smelly, small, and leaning toward diabetes. He had recently started to view his body as a pair of handcuffs, holding him down, humiliating him, keeping him from really enjoying himself.

He was glad to be free of it.

The transition had actually been pretty easy. The stabbing pain in his elbow, the wave of concussion, a moment of darkness, light, and then flames. But he didn't feel the fire. All Robert felt was...nothing. He was in a great ball of angry flames, watching the roof of the apartment building rush towards and then through him and all he felt was a sense of expansion.

Oh, my God, he thought—his mind blooming beyond the usual confines of his brain. *Oh, my God,* he thought as the flames roaring up from the collapsed roof danced around and through him. No pain, no real sensation. He seemed to just be there, watching the fire, listening to it eat the wood and plaster. *I think I'm here,* he thought. *I think I have hands. I think I still have something like a body.*

The fire started to make him uncomfortable. He still didn't feel anything, but the sight of the flames licking away at the building scared him—because he couldn't feel it.

So he left. *Oh, my God,* Ruge thought as he hovered over the burning building and looked down at the gawkers, the arriving fire engines, his body in the street, the fireflies of embers, the thick churning clouds of smoke. Slowly, as he watched and grew strangely accustomed to it all, he became aware that he did have a body.

It was the one he always knew he had.

He was strong. Looking around, he saw himself take form. Muscles shimmered and coalesced. His hands were wide and long. His arms had become semitransparent bundles of strength. His legs were thick columns of silvery muscle. He couldn't see it, but he knew that his face was lantern-jawed, with a cleft chin, brilliant eyes, and a cascade of midnight hair hanging in a negative halo around his powerful skull (after all, he was floating). This was the Ruge that lived in the meat—the man inside.

I'm here, he thought. I'm finally here.

Ruge was happy. He was strong. He was well-defined. He was Tom of Finland. He soared through the fading flames, phased through the billowing black clouds of smoke and steam, and flashed through pigeons. The weight of his ugly body was gone. His flesh lay in the street among the wreckage of the building and the frantic firemen.

No one had told the young Robert Ruge that coming to the City, coming out, and jumping in, would make him happy. No one had misled him—but there was always a part of him that felt like a promise hadn't been kept. He had come out, moved to Sodom by the Sea, and jumped into the sparkling depths of the Polk Gulch. For a while he was part of a world that loved him and thought him sexy.

Then gravity. Then male pattern baldness. *Troll* used to be giggles and snickers, pointing to someone else. After a few very short years it was a sarcastic self-definition.

Some took it on as a kind of kink. Some hung up their hats and tried to find the same to grow old with.

In his cell, with masturbation and *American Gladiators,* R. Ruge seethed and hated.

Now, though, he was free. He was big and strong and huge—where it mattered. He was free and beautiful, now that he was dead.

And he wasn't alone.

The two dykes shot past him—bound for some kind of Valhalla, no doubt—fused into a churning ball of brilliant light, their lust and love consuming them and turning them into a kind of afterlife comet. Mr. Skila hovered over the steaming wreckage of his building, his own form like a kind of long-limbed gazelle or antelope: weirdly stretched arms and legs; a narrow, ribbed chest; and a streamlined head. Ruge suddenly remembered that Mr. Skila only seemed to sparkle when the Bay to Breakers poured down their street. Dead, Mr. Skila could run and run and run for all eternity.

The kid who worked in the java joint churned overhead—a great clockwork mandala spinning around and through and over itself in a dizzying display of convolutions and articulations. Too much of everything. Too many perceptions altered from high school till Mr. Skila's match tore his body apart. The kid who worked in the java joint was now really free to explore the limits of perception.

Then there was the other one.

He floated up from the remains of the now-smoldering apartment, filling Robert's vision with his perfection—a Roman statue stepping from its pedestal, a Greek god striding away from his column. Big, broad shoulders, a chest of well-defined (if spectral) muscles, legs like pillars of stone, and a face that was strong yet lit by emotion. Eyes that danced with desire and fire. Michelangelo's David—the man in 1A.

They were in love. It was an almost perfect match.

The attraction was magnetic, electric—sparks flew as they grew closer and touched. It was that moment—the one when attraction meets attraction. You find him hot; he finds you hot. Mutual polarity of pure lust. They touched, hands first, and felt the current flow between them. Their eyes took each other in, sized each other up, and found very little lacking.

They had a lot of the earth still about them. Their bodies, for instance, and certainly what their bodies did when they found each other attractive.

Slightly startled by this, they both looked down between them at the gauges of their attraction and laughed.

In his flesh, R. Ruge was a piggy-dicked man. When it was hard it was small and turned obviously to the left. The shaft was narrow and his circumcised head was ridiculously bulbous. Dead, his cock was spectral iron, a great jutting spear—shaft wide and strong, tapering to a perfectly proportioned head. Between them, his cock was up and ready at a 45-degree angle.

And as they danced, touching and floating above the building, Ruge rubbed against the cock of the man in 1A. David's wasn't maybe as pronounced and exaggerated, but it was just about perfect. It was one of those cocks that stops your breath—not huge, not monstrous, just...beautiful. Ruge found himself staring at it, watching it bob and weave between then, grazing his own every once and a while—sparks flying as a tense precome wave washed through him.

Ghosts, they kissed, pressing the cocks they deserved between them. It was more than their new bodies that held them together, they knew. They were just about made for each other. They kissed with lightning, feeling their tongues spark and entwine and grapple like twin magnets. They rubbed and held each other close, feeling their cocks press against their bellies (and against nipples, in the case of Ruge's member). They humped and laughed and screamed with joy at their new playthings. David laughed and clapped his strong, supple mouth over Ruge's bulbous cock head and sucked and surged raw voltage through them, connecting them, negative pole to positive pole, linked and joined, mouth to cock. Free of cruel gravity, Ruge flipped himself over and completed the circuit with a spectral sixty-nine that lit the skies of San Francisco like a lovely summer storm.

Free now to do whatever they wanted, they did just that. Ruge took the god from behind, easing himself into an asshole that was more than just a place to shit from. David's asshole was a portal, a door into him. As Ruge went in and out in a great cosmic butt fuck, David's asshole surged and sparked and twirled around his new cock like a particle accelerator. They weren't fucking with tissues and muscle and cartilage, they were fucking with ectoplasm, electrons, protons, and quarks. When they came, and they did and did and did, they came with ghostly subatomic explosions.

David put his semitransparent hand around Ruge's new cock and seemed to lose himself. Ruge, in turn, became lost in the sensation of David's strong and sparking hand. Ruge became everything he ever wanted to be—the object of pure lust.

Then it was Ruge's turn to receive. While not as grandiose as Ruge's cock, David's was more finely conceived. While not filling him until it tapped against his back teeth, David's cock did fill exactly where it needed to fill. It was an almost perfect fit. It pushed every good button Ruge had. It churned his sex from the inside out. It flowed through his asshole, around his heart, and down through his own throbbing cock. It tickled around the edges of his soul and the boundaries of his Self. It was a key that

Ruge knew would unlock the absolutely most beautiful orgasms of his existence.

Then Ruge was in pain, lying on the sidewalk. Someone was saying "One, two, three—clear!"

Coarse voltage slammed into him, and his teeth snapped down hard enough to chip a molar. His leg screamed in pain from where it had been sheared off at the knee. His face felt like it had been ground away. His skin felt like it was still burning. It felt like needles and soldering irons lay across him or pierced his bleeding body.

R. Ruge was alive again.

The paramedic injected something into his arm. It felt like a red hot fireplace poker being shoved through him. His scream echoed through his skull and bounced around inside the oxygen mask strapped to his face. Somewhere, someone said something about a drug, but another voice said something about the possibility of shock and a weak heart.

R. Ruge was awake. His eyes darted, seeing the fading smoke from the fire, the hurried looks from the paramedics fleeting in and out of his range of vision. Behind them, above them, he could still see the angel David, the man in room 1A, hovering, longing, desiring. They were so close, but there was so much between them—now.

It was too much. The pain. The taking away of all he had ever wanted—no, deserved. David was what he deserved above all else. A lifetime of rage and selfishness and self-pity and destruction boiled up and through his shattered and burned body and for a split second he didn't feel anything except pure hatred for everyone and everything.

The small oxygen bottle was lying against his arm. He could feel its slight coolness through his first- and second-degree burns. With the strength of hatred at all those who had lived so much when he had been jailed in his failing body, he lifted the bottle and smashed it across the face of the nearest paramedic.

He lost consciousness again shortly after that. When next he awoke, he was laying in a hospital bed—the beeping, dripping attendants of medical science keeping him alive and in incredible pain. Most of that day was gone, erased by whatever cruelty it is that makes us forget dreams. One thing, and one thing only, remained, an image that hung over him: of the paramedic leaving his own body and traveling up and away from the street, away from R. Ruge and the fire. There the paramedic met David, the man in 1A, and they flew off to an absolutely perfect, perfect, match. They had been really, truly, made for each other—they weren't an almost perfect match.

They were a perfect match.

Casey, the Bat

The ballpark was a riot of sensoria. Nothing would stay fixed, would stick in the mind—there was just too much. Overload. A picture a thousand words? Try a thousand pictures, a hundred thousand pictures. Not enough words, anywhere, ever written, to describe the park that day.

Till, that is, Barrows was thrown out at first. The second out of the inning. Then just one word would suffice—a singular word that hovered, heavy and absolute—at least in the confines of the park: Like the sweet stink of lemonade, the buttery crispness of popcorn, the meaty tang of hot dogs, the bitter mist of fresh cans of beer hissing open on that afternoon, failure was in the air.

A scattered few, having lost the faith, bowed their heads and slipped away, as if sneaking from church when the vicar started reading hellfire—not wanting to see Mudville's shame roared from the stands.

The crowd, however, roared its approval as Flynn let drive a single. Then Blake tore the cover off the ball, and together they ran down the white lines. When the dust had settled and everyone saw what had occurred, there was Blake safe at second and Flynn a-hugging third.

Cataclysm! A bellowing roar from the beast of hope, a throaty call from thousands, an echoing rumble that bounced up the hilltops and down the dells. The noise broke, forming sounds the ear could hear, the mind comprehend—a chanting cry: "Casey! Casey! Casey! Casey!"

But then the sound died down, fading into the dying afternoon. The batter's box lay empty, the team looked confused: Casey, where was Casey? Now that it was almost his turn at the plate...

The sound bounced and warped and turned and flew, but down it couldn't quite reach, down it couldn't quite go...to Casey. Casey, he was otherwise detained. Down in the Mudville locker room the sound couldn't reach, but even if it had, even if it could, it was doubtful that Casey, the Mighty Casey, would have heard.

For Casey, Mighty Casey, was down there...and at bat.

Rogers was at second, his great member inflamed and hard, stroking it slow and steady in and out of Casey's mouth; and Martin was at home, tremendous dick pumping hard, pumping fast in Casey's so-tight ass.

Fernandez was on first, cock pulsing in Casey's mighty fist; and Jones was at third, his long, thin member wrapped tight in Casey's mitt.

Casey, Mighty Casey, the pride of the Mudville nine, moaned a freight train's dirge as if lumbering up some insane hill—a bellowing of pleasure, a bull's roar of straining pleasure as cocks slid in and out, pistons hammering in fleshy engines from his mouth, his ass. In accompaniment, in perfect balancing performance, two great members were also in his sweaty palms, and he stroked them—did Mighty Casey—as he was fucked from in front and behind.

Fans, yes, they would have been stricken—shocked and

ashamed—at this side of their Casey, uniform around his ankles, asshole all inflamed. But not for his activity would they be so disappointed, not for his mouth sucking, asshole fucking would they be outraged. No, their curses, their anger, their fear wouldn't be for the man love of their Mighty Casey—for many such things were simple Saturday nights, ways of passing the country hours, something to do that was as much a pastime as sitting in the stands watching their beloved Mudville nine. They would be displeased not in the activity taking place that summer day, but in the fact that Casey, Mighty Casey, was doing it with the other team.

"Casey! Casey! Casey! Casey!" Their cheers increased, now echoing down the concrete tunnels, making a perfect music for the sucking and fucking there. "Casey!"—as dick slid down Casey's throat, hairy balls smacking into his drool-slicked chin, fat cock head tickling the back of his throat, whispering gag to him, but ignored in the joy of dick in mouth. "Casey!"—as cock hammered back and forth, in and out, to and fro in his puckered asshole, nether lips wrapped around long muscle, milking come from a so-hard member. "Casey!"—as the Mighty pulled, stroked, twisted, pulled, yanked at the cock in his right hand. "Casey!"—as he did the same to the other in his left, feeling it jump and throb in his hand with each motion, each action.

"Casey! Casey!"

The coach, the dear coach, of the Mudville nine was wont to say that a team is not just men together, but men together acting as one man. Casey, the star of the team, the man to whom the other Mudville players looked up with respect and awe, would have agreed—a team working well is one man, and that day, in that locker room, Casey and those men were one man: a man with a great throbbing dick; a man with a pulsing, gripping asshole; a man with lips straining around cock flesh, swallowing meat; a man with his cock in a hand and sometimes a mouth; a man with his hands on many cocks. They were a squirming, fucking, sucking unit down there in the Mudville locker room that day. The coach would have been proud of their unity, their grace of movement, their passion for the game, though he too would have been distressed over Casey's choice in playmates.

In and out, in and out, the machine of men worked—fluids of pleasure dropping with heavy weight to the tough concrete floor. Come and spit, spit and drool slicked the floor, made it gleam. A well-oiled machine, a slick and salty engine of pumping and being pumped, an athletic performance of the highest caliber.

"Casey! Casey!"

As a single mechanism they moved, they worked, they played. As a single unit they plunged, stroked, sucked, licked, and all of that, together, combined. To the pounding chorus of a stadium demanding, hammering, and cheering for their mighty hero, the gleaming Casey and his rivals churned and rocked, moved and moaned. Cocks in hand, cock in mouth, cock in ass—fucking, getting fucked, the locker room rang with the meaty slap of flesh in and on flesh. To that thunderous cheer of hope and praise, Casey, Mighty Casey, got reamed and sucked, fucked and done by the dreaded, and very hard, bats of the other team.

Then, there, with his name on all those lips and his cock in a single set, the coming came. Jets, spurts, and sprays. Quakes, quivers, and gushers. Geysers, splashes, and earthquakes. Sweet, sticky ejaculate erupted from four iron dicks, cascading onto Casey's, Mighty Casey's, perfectly honed muscles, shaking as his own brilliant orgasm blasted fireworks and rang loud gongs in his ears.

Coming, coming, coming, they came—jizz and sweat, salt and sweet, mixed in their valleys and creases. It leaked from firm lips, trickled from a puckered asshole, dropped from between shivering fingers.

"Casey! Casey!"

The thunder above mixed with their thunder below—a booming applause to the power of man juice, the blasting eruption of orgasm.

Sleep reached up and grabbed hold of Casey—a heavy, soft weight promising rest, promising dreams. But something intruded, and despite his aching muscles, his draining strength, the great man pushed—ah, but gently—his playmates aside, listening with half an ear to the exhausted, meaty impacts of their tired bodies hitting the too-hard floor.

"Casey! Casey! Casey! Casey!"

Into his garments he struggled, arms into sleeves, legs into legs. As the other team slipped, collapsed into a Goya tableau of exhaustion, their trained muscles sprung by the rapid release of joy, the legend climbed a small, personal mountain...by climbing into his uniform.

"Casey! Casey! Casey! Casey!" came their prayer, their chant, their worship—a thousand feet stamping, a thousand hands clapping, a thousand Mudvillians screaming for their baseball savior, their batting messiah, to appear.

Then, emerging after what seemed like three days—and what certainly felt like resurrection—he came, a smile broad and true on his lips, a swagger in his mighty hips, a great bat resting on his shoulder, up from the darkness and into the light.

A riot before, revival after. The crowd rose in salute as Casey, Mighty Casey, stepped onto the field. True, the odds were against them, the game looked lost, but hope was magic, and love for Casey all. Their cheer at his arrival was the joyous noise of hope.

Casey allowed their adoration to drum around him, humbly doffing his cap in a return salute, turning to see them all and allow them all to see, before raising a great hand to bring the sound down, down, down to the softness of subtle whispers of confidence.

Confidence, yes, because while the odds were against them and the game all but lost, Casey, Mighty Casey, had stepped up to the plate.

Swinging his bat—no, gentle reader, not the one that just minutes before had been serviced by the other team—he glanced cool intent at the pitcher on the mound, as if daring him to throw anything his way, let alone the ball.

"Strike one!" came the umpire's call as the catcher caught the throw. The crowd was stunned, aghast, but Casey was still strong. They saw this in their hero, the legend of their town, and still they cheered him, rooted him on.

"Strike two!" was the second cry as the ball smacked into the catcher's mitt. *What is this?* the fans seemed to say. *What could this mean?* Was Casey, their Mighty Casey, going to let them down?

Ah, but faith is a powerful thing, and their hope only wavered, but did not fall. As the pitcher spun his arm, took deadly aim, the crowd bellowed out the crack, the screaming hit, long before great Casey swung his bat. They saw the ball go flying, they saw it sail away. They knew their hero, the Great and Noble Casey, had saved the day—and the game—again.

"Strike three!" What was this? Their aghast and denial a thunderous cry—Casey had missed. Slowly, so very slowly, they realized this for truth: that Casey, Mighty Casey, had struck out.

For the Mudville fans that day, the game was over, a winner's joy not theirs. Slowly they walked with sorrowful steps into the chilly night, sadness anchoring them to the harsh, cruel world. No smiles on their lips, no cheer from their throats, for Casey, their once-mighty Casey, had let them down.

But what of their once-hero, the legend of the bat? He, you see, dear reader, was nowhere to be found. Not in the club, not on the street, not in the bars, and not at his home. Their Casey had gone, vanished without a trace, and his absence, with the loss of the game, weighed heavily on Mudville that day.

Sadness, though, was not completely the order of the day. For Casey, Mighty Casey, was merely back in that locker room, smiling broad and wide, at bat once again, taking and delivering in asshole, mouth, and hand. One game over, maybe a defeat, but another just beginning—where everyone would win.

So there was, at least for Mighty Casey, some joy in Mudville that day.

Chickenhawk

It didn't start out as a good night—still pretty fucked up from that bad spill I took the week before. My knee kept shooting out from under me, so it was damned hard to stay on the skateboard. Probably added a good degree of charm, though: me trying to balance against my fucked-up knee and crashing again and again on the grass and every once in a while on the damned sidewalk. The only real trick was trying to keep my fucking mouth shut, or at least to whimper out a pained "Ohhh, fuck," and not what I fucking wanted to say, in my full, real, loud voice.

It was a prime time, in a prime spot—a triangle of boring green in a forgotten cul-de-sac of a third-rate suburb. A squiggle of hard sidewalk, a sandpit more like a giant litter box for stray cats than a playground accessory, a pair of broken swings hanging like strung-up horse-thieves, and a mass of pipe and cheap-ass fiberglass some hustler had called a "play structure" and sold to the bland, planned tract.

The sun was mostly gone, leaving a hard, red glow on the fake red-tile roofs of the houses—about an hour from the sodium streetlights coming on. At this hour, kids with careful, watching parents were inside, eating dinner or watching reruns of *The Simpsons*. But the trash kids, the ones who wouldn't be missed for most of the night, were still out trying to fucking ride their fucking piece-of-shit skateboards. Prime time. Prime spot. But no nibbles.

I was about to pack it in when the shitty red Toyota cruised by for the second time. He wasn't craning to see house numbers, and there were plenty of parking places.

Fuck, I wanted a drag. Wouldn't fit the look, though. Besides, mine were in my car, three blocks away. I'd have to crave. Could've used a drink, too.

I was in my usual duds: trashed knees, messed hair, denim cut offs that just begged for it, and a stinky, threadbare T-shirt. Today it was my black Metallica—nothing like a cliché to string along other clichés. I looked like the runaway poster boy.

I tried my best to look hideously bored as he circled one more time. *Come on*, I thought, trying not to look as fucking impatient as I felt. *Don't cruise him; let him cruise you.*

Finally: "Hey, you know the way to Mangrove street?" he said, leaning across the passenger seat and spastically rolling down the window. He was old—no shit—maybe 50, 45 at least. Gray hair like a flock of gulls had the runs on his head, pulled across to hide a bald spot. Brown shirt buttoned way up to his neck. He didn't look big, definitely didn't look rough. Didn't tell me dick, though, with his inane question—except that he was interested.

I shrugged. "It's way over there," I said, pointing vaguely to the right. "Past the Army base."

He looked concerned. "I've got to get there in a few minutes," he said, "Got a meeting with the manager of the Crescent."

He'd scoped the savanna at least, done his research—either that or he was local. The Crescent was the town's only real club, and someone like me would be impressed that he was going there—let alone having a meeting with the manager.

"Cool," I said, grabbing my board, getting up, walking to the car. "The Crescent's cool."

"I guess so," he said, sounding bored, but his face shined with nervousness. "I'm supposed to get down there and book the Strays. I'm their road man."

Body wasn't hip, but his shtick sure was: The Strays were hot but not too big, and road man wasn't manager. Impressive, but not over the top.

"Cool!" I said, hopping up and down. "The Strays are mega-cool!"

"Don't know myself, kid. I just book them, you know? So, hey, how the hell do I get over there?"

"Well..." I said, taking a long time to formulate an answer, showing that I wasn't too quick. "It's really far. You have to get over to the turnpike and then get off on this one street. It's by the Piggly Wiggly."

"Hey, look, why you just get in and show me where? I'll get you back in no time. Besides, I'm sure I've got some Strays stuff in the trunk I can give you. Shirts, posters, some CDs, you know."

I pondered. He's interested, hard in his brown corduroys. He's dropped the worm and he's waiting for the twitch. He's scanning the street for someone watching, noticing the kid leaning in his passenger window. So was I: no need for a concerned parent to get interested in us.

"Sure, I guess so. I've got to be home by 9, though." Two hours, plenty of time.

"No problem." He popped the door and couldn't resist patting the passenger seat next to him. I flopped down.

"Where can I put my board?"

"Just toss it in the back." He practically left rubber as he made his dash out of there. Man, he was hard for me. Very nice, I thought. Leave the brain behind and follow your little head.

Ten minutes: "What's your name, anyway?"

"Brian."

"I'm Stu. You live around here, Brian?"

"Over on Rosemont. Three fifty-three."

We were quiet for a while. Then: "How old are you, Brian?"

"Fifteen." Every once and a while I have to up it by a year—skin doesn't pass, voice won't crackle like it used to. Fifteen is good, about as low as I could pull off but still be juicy, tempting.

He's not a pro, but he's got the moves—direct without being pushy, laid-back and paternal instead of drooling and hungry. Made it look natural, flowing. No candy, no dirty pictures. Still, each is his own, got his own plans at the end. No way of knowing until you get there. I didn't know if I'd have to use the razor in my shoe or the needle stuck in my belt.

"Aw, fuck!" he said, thumping the steering wheel. Upset but not berserk, angry but not frightening. "Forgot my schedule sheets. Hang on." Then he pulled off, using an exit only a local would know. Three or four turns later we were on a dark street. Trucks in yards, batteries next to overflowing trash cans, leaves everywhere. Dogs barked, claiming territories only they would want.

The house sat way back, hidden by a misshapen old tree. The leaves on the ground were half a foot thick, covering what I guessed might be a lawn. The few house numbers I could see were faded almost to invisibility. I also noticed that the street sign was gone: He probably made sure of that whenever the city put a new one up. Slip out and you'd have a hard time finding the place again, at least in a hurry.

"Wanna come in for a sec? I've got some cool Strays stuff from their last tour."

I shrugged again, covering the excitement at hanging with the

Strays' road man with some good rocker boredom. "Sure."

Inside: clean but not spotless, more empty than neat. As he walked in I put my finger on my belt, feeling the electrical tape-wrapped end of my six-inch spring steel needle. Mostly these guys work alone, but you never can tell. As he opened the door, I quick-scanned the living room and kitchen: normal city. Shit-ugly gold couch. Entertainment center with a five-year-old TV. Blank, unlabeled video tapes. Kitchen with a counter and two unused barstools. Sliding door to a backyard choked with dead, yellow weeds—and a single tire swing. That creeped me, down deep, and made me look harder at the guy. Something about that swing made me rethink his age interests.

He was five-eight and his shoulders spoke of tension strength, probably humming with hormones. His ass, in those fucking ugly brown cords, was loose and flabby, though. He probably couldn't move all that fast.

Secrets. I knew the front room without really having to look that hard at it. I knew the real rooms were in the back. Den with some more tapes, maybe a camera or two. Maybe some journals, diaries, but for sure a box of items—had to learn about the Crescent and the Strays from somewhere.

"You want a drink?" he said, walking into the kitchen, going to the fridge and taking out two Buds. He popped them on the counter—behind a pillar so I couldn't see.

I didn't need to. I just hoped he used something I knew. It was hard enough dealing with their shit when you knew what to expect and the walls weren't breathing.

He gave me a beer as I checked out the room, the way an impressed 15-year-old would. "Cool," I said, knocking back a hefty swig.

"Hey," he said, moving quickly to the tapes and the TV, "I think I've got Metallica's latest concert here somewhere—all kinds of stuff that didn't make it into their video."

"Cool!" I said for the sixth or seventh nauseating time. God, I fucking hated 15-year-olds. It was a lot more fun a few years back when I could pull off 9 and 10. Crying worked great then— but I also had to pack something more nasty than just the razor and the wire. "Uh, I gotta use the bathroom."

"Right through here," he said, guiding me to one door, steering me away from the others. File cabinets, collection box, *the bedroom*?

He hung around like he wanted me to invite him in. I almost did, but no 15-year-old worth hunting would ever do that. So I started to close the door and that gave him his clue to back off toward the living room.

Five…four…three…two…one…when I was sure he was gone, nervously selecting a tape to "accidentally" show me, I stuck a finger down my throat and chucked up what little of the beer I'd slugged. Then I poured the rest out and filled it with cold water. Just to add to the effect, and because I really had to, I pissed and flushed before walking out.

I didn't know what was in the beer, can't tell those things from the taste. Probably Valium or X, though—the spices of choice. Probably Valium. X was a little too hip for this guy, who obviously scored his info from MTV and his other "guests." When I came out I drooped just enough for him to relax.

Metallica was, indeed, on—probably taped from MTV. He sat on the couch, watching the show and not me. I sat with just enough space between us. Just enough to show the spice had taken effect and that I wasn't creeped and that I was maybe even comfortable.

When I turned 18 and had to start working it was hard, as only everything can be when you're 18 but only 4-foot-8. Security guard? Right. Modeling? Store clerk? Office worker? Fuck that noise. Who wants to hire someone who looks nine? So I hustled. One time, early on, I thought this guy was picking me up for a usual trick, or an *unusual* trick—into dwarfs, you know. Then I finally realized, with old-man lips on my dick, that he thought I was a kid. A little kid. That freaked me. I played having to go to the bathroom and slipped out a window. Fucked up my ankle falling to the street.

It didn't take long for me to figure out my career. I was bait: 13 on the outside, 30 on the inside. You just gotta find your niche, I guess.

Sure enough, halfway into the concert, the porno came on. I'd seen it already. Another of those Jeff Stryker things. I hate that fucker. I mean, when you're my size, seeing a dick the size of a baseball bat ravaging some poor guy's asshole can really make you nervous. It's all a matter of proportion: baseball bat for that guy, telephone pole for me.

At least it wasn't kiddie porn. I can't stand that trip. Happens too often too. Good feeling afterward, though. Righteous the morning after. Still, I hadn't checked out his office or bedroom yet, so I didn't know how the night would end.

"Oh, damn" he said, obviously pissed off at either himself or someone else. Like he'd really forgotten he'd taped over Metallica with Jeff Stryker video, or like someone had sneaked in and done it to him.

I knew he'd be watching me, so I just watched the screen, trying for all my worth not to squirm with boredom.

His body heat invaded my space so I took another drink of my beer. His hand went to my leg. "Come on, man," I said in a slow motion voice.

I tried a little harder when his hand landed on my half-hard dick. "Come on, don't." If he had stopped then I would've ended up doing something else, like dropping my voice and just kicking the shit out of him. But he didn't, and his moist paw started kneading me hard.

His breath, at least, wasn't foul, as he hunted for my mouth. I turned away. Kissing is one of the few things I won't do—and never with these guys. Something about getting that fucking close to their teeth, as if cock sucking wasn't bad enough. Don't know why, but we've all got lines, I guess that's one of mine: I don't have to explain if I don't want to.

He took my beer away, put it on this piece-of-crap coffee table, and started working my cutoffs down, gabbing all the time like a drunk on the DTs trying to shoo away the pink elephants: "It's gonna be OK. It really is. there's nothing to be afraid of. It's going to feel really nice, I swear. I mean it. You like good things, right? Well, this is one of the best. I mean it, I really do. It'll be great. Just don't cry..."

I struggled a bit, mostly so I could slide my needle out—easily reachable if I needed it. Then I put on my 'lude mask and tried to fumble him away with no tension in my muscles, muttering a very insincere, "No way, don't." It's tricky: struggle, but not too hard. It's no fun if he stops.

Finally the creep got my dick in his mouth. I was only half hard, but he had enthusiasm on his side. Nothing but warm, soft tissues draped over me and in a couple of beats of my heart I was swollen hard in his mouth. No pro, this creep, but at least he didn't seem to have learned all his cock sucking from Jeff Stryker flicks: He was really hungry for dick—baby dick, kid dick, but at least that's all he seemed to want. Sucked like he expected gold or fucking champagne to come out. He sucked in his cheeks so I could feel the silken insides of his mouth slide and graze along my shaft and head. Then he gave the back of his throat a couple of taps with my cock head, knocking to tell it to open up, I guess.

Sometimes they stop at this point, or maybe when they first

get my pants down, looking hard at my face and body and then at my cock—way too big. My cock is one of the few things on me that actually grew since I really was 15. God giveth, God taketh away. But this guy obviously thought he'd just scored the fucking mother lode of 15-year-old boys.

I wish I wasn't cut, but some things you can't fake. Still, I like it when the fat edges of my cock head graze teeth—like with this guy. Good feeling when done well and, creep or no, he did it well. Up, down, around, and tickle. His tongue played me as he pistoned up and down in my lap, milking me like there was no tomorrow, like I was the present he'd waited years for.

Well, this jailbait was happy to accommodate. He even used the ridges along the roof of his mouth to add vibration to his sucking. Nice. I groaned for him, remembering to crack my voice.

Yeah, damned fucking enthusiastic. The fat end of my cut dick tickled his tonsils and I felt his throat softly balloon open in prep for taking me all the way down. He lay on his side now, with his head in my lap and his own ugly-as-shit pants around his ankles. His whistling (fucking annoying) breathing through his nose tickled my pubes and made my balls cold. I tried real hard not to look at his tiny dick as he flicked it with two fingers. It was hard, which was sad, because I'd seen gerbils better hung.

Still, I wasn't going to do anything with it. I moaned pretty convincingly—mainly because I really was getting off. OK, give the creep some points; at least he got my skinny ass hard and throbbing. Just the right combo of tongue, palate, and throat. Fucking, fucking, *sucking* good. Still, I kept my hand on my needle—just in case velvet had teeth, or worse, buried somewhere in the future—while I fished out the Rohypnol tablet I had taped inside my shirt.

I actually creamed for the fucker. I was so shocked I almost laughed out loud and did something stupid like ruffle his hair like I would with a regular trick. I started to cry, instead, and slap at his head. No consent, not me. That's the gauge, the game. Back off and the evening would end different. Don't and ... it's a helluva lot more fun—but just for me.

I kicked over my beer. He jerked away and I scrambled to get my pants up and give him a major hard time: "Goddamned fucking homo asshole," I wailed through burning tears, shoving him away hard enough to make him rear back. I dropped forward, scrambling to recover my beer, at the same time sliding my hand right over his beer and dropping in the tab.

Funny how this works: Stick someone in a really difficult position, make a drink handy, and they'll usually take a sip, just to have something, anything to do.

He did. Sometimes I have to use the needle or the razor if they don't. But this guy was true to form.

I cried more and more while he did his act, playing guilt over his face between earnest gulps of beer, waiting for me to get over my fit so he could offer a bribe or a nice, cold threat.

I kept it up a while longer than he was comfortable with, getting him good and pissed. Nothing like that to get the old blood flowing, pumping from guts to brain, speeding the reaction.

Sure as shit: *Bam!* He dropped like a sack, legs out straight, slid right off the couch to sprawl between it and the coffee table. I knew he was still kind of awake—tried the stuff myself once—but too fucking whacked to move. He'd stay that way for a long time and wake up with no memory of me, our fun, or *my* fun.

I got up, adjusted my pants and rubbed my sore knee—I'd given it another righteous twist when I flopped off the couch. I checked the creep's pulse—quick but OK—and then the rest of the house.

Two bald tires, some grease-crusted tools, a broken wheelbarrow, boxes of old *Reader's Digest* condensed books and

National Geographic magazines in the garage. The backyard was hard as fucking cement, no fresh dirt. The office had more boxes of *National Geographic*, a couple of kiddie porn magazines, and a Bible. The rest was shit-ugly clothes in black plastic bags. The bedroom had a too-soft mattress on a creaky box spring with a set of cheap, hotel-special sheets. More bags of clothes (all his size). I pulled a pillowcase off and used it as a glove to check under the bed—more magazines and a big-ass dildo. No diary. No cameras. Found a stash of 700 bucks in a coffee can in the closet. Went into my pocket.

I went back into the living room and carefully checked out his tapes. Most of them were standard Stryker-type stuff—handsome studs taking it and giving it to each other. Nothing younger than mainstream teenage guys, who were probably in college and needed the bucks.

Nothing so bad—but all bad enough.

I checked him again. Still breathing. I grabbed his wallet.

I cleaned the place—wiping everything I'd touched—and put the kiddie stuff in the front room. I grabbed some oily rags and a can of fire starter from the garage. The rags went against an interior wall and the fire starter went fucking everywhere. Then I called the cops, making my voice high and squealing, breaking with panic, giving them the story with a different ending: how I managed to knock him out (but not before he raped me). They said to stay on the line, so I dropped the phone, lit the big pool of fire starter, and walked out the door. Five blocks away I passed a parade of three cop cars, screaming toward that unmarked but now dully glowing street.

He'd been a good cocksucker. That saved him. That and not enough shit to hang him with. A little more—some pictures, souvenirs, soft earth in the backyard, even a slap, and I would have whacked him then and there. That, or tied him down good, carved him up some, and then not called the cops before I tossed the match.

It was a two-hour walk back to my car. When I got back I changed into my civvies (one of the benefits of being my size, you can change your clothes in a parked car with ease) and drove back to my motel.

Not a bad score. One less of "them," and about a grand and four credit cards I could sell for a hundred each.

Tomorrow, I thought, I'll hang out at the arcade—do a little fishing, and see if I can beat my high score.

What Ails You

"He was mean." It was the way Darrin said it, with a catch in his voice, a wound somewhere deep down that lovely throat. "He said I was a doll, but I'd lost my porcelain shine." Pure Tennessee Williams. Pure Darrin. What the freak had probably said was that Darrin wasn't up to his standards, maybe called him "a flaming screamer with bad lipstick."

It wasn't that that bothered Lion, and it wasn't Darrin's tears either—because Darrin cried when the setting sun seemed to set New Orleans aflame. No, what set Lion's blood to boiling was the smear of blood running from Darrin's nose to his chin.

"He was not an honorable gentleman," Darrin said, smiling up at Lion and sniffling softy as he dabbed at the blood with one of Lion's fine silk handkerchiefs.

Honorable, no. Seriously fucked, yes, Lion thought, leaning against the alley wall, bricks leaving red dust on his fine blue suit. "You don't worry none about it, D," Lion said, reaching into his pocket for a smoke. "It's none of your concern now." His Zippo flashed and the smoke from his elegant European cigarette added a redolent fragrance to the rot and piss smell of the alley.

"But he started out as such a good trick. Said he wanted it a little rough—and you know I can do that, Leo." Darrin was one of the few of Lion's who got away with calling him Leo. "And I did a good job. You know, a little 'On your knees, cocksucker, and prove you're one.' Maybe a little spanky spanky and some fun with his chute. I know the game, Leo. I'm good at it, you know I am. He was just a little meaner than usual, that's all."

Lion bent down and cupped Darrin's face, tilted it up carefully to look into his eyes. "I said this is none of your concern. You just clean yourself up and take in a show or something. Maxine's working The 87 Club, maybe you two can get a drink." Lion's black face was all but invisible in the night of the alley, but his polished and shining white and gold teeth flashed stray city lights.

Lion moved back against the brick wall of the alley and Darrin got up to go.

"He's at the Front Street."

"I know," Lion said, taking a pull on his cigarette, showing his face in the dull red glow.

He was in room 414. The beatnik bellhop took Lion's ten-spot and nodded slowly, leaking out that he was there now and that the hotel wasn't full. His room might very well be the only one occupied on the fourth floor.

Lion knew the Front very well. Fancy French glass doors. Brass. Knew the bellhop was reliable, that its walls were thick and absorbent of sounds (perfect for his business, when the customers got really excited). The Front was one of the classier hangs for his "girls," and he made sure that the ones who staked out its guests in the Green Room across the street were the best of his stable. Darrin was the top: quick, clean, and smooth—silk. He knew the game and knew the act. Now Darrin would be out of it for two, maybe three days. Longer if the freak had hurt him worse than Darrin let on. That was money gone. That was his rep getting hurt—that he couldn't take care of his girls.

Besides, Darrin could suck the cream from your coffee. Lion actually liked the little queen.

Knew the Front *very* well. The back door to the service stairs was always unlocked. Room 414 was just around the corner.

Lion knocked once.

The door opened. The freak almost said, "Yes?" before Lion sent him spinning into the bed. The man hit hard and sloppy, back against the iron bed frame, his flailing right arm slapping against a low-hanging ceiling fan. By the time he had recovered enough of his senses to know he'd been hit, Lion had calmly checked the hall for witnesses, stepped into the room, and closed the door quietly behind him

The guy wasn't that old, and that was surprising. Eight years of working his girls and being their Man had given him a pretty clear picture of how things worked. And someone mouthing off and ruffing one of his girls didn't jive with a youngish guy. It fit a slug, a leech, a guy who thought that because his daddy was white and his mommy was white and his family had always lived in the South he had special "dispensations" against niggers and queers—even if he liked to have his cock sucked by the best of them.

A bad customer was something that happened. It was something that happened less to Lion's girls, though—because of Lion's voice when he said "You take good care of him" to the clients as well as to the girls; or because Lion was a giant, a huge muscled gentleman of color and refinement who could bend quarters between thumb and forefinger.

Also because of his *cure.*

"Get up," Lion said to the man in 414. When the man didn't, just kept leaning back against the bed and panting heavily, Lion reached down and grabbed him by the back of the neck and hauled him up.

"You is shit, is what you is," Lion said. "You ain't a man, you ain't a gentleman, you ain't even a client. You is nothing but shit."

The guy looked at Lion with quivering brown eyes. His face was surprisingly fine and hard. He looked like someone you'd maybe see working high steel somewhere: strong and firm but light enough for climbing. That hard, planed face spoke of Indian blood, maybe, or something Mexican. Not heavy, though, just an accent. His skin had the dimness of a short-sleeve tan. Farmer's tan. Telephone man? Railroad man? He was good enough overall to get it otherwise. A part of Lion puzzled over this. You didn't see this kind much in street business.

Only a part of Lion puzzled over this; a much larger part smelled the man's fear. And it made him hard. Very hard.

The man was practically shaking.

"You came to me for a service, to borrow something of mine. Then you damage what is *mine.* That is inconsiderate. Very inconsiderate."

The slap sounded like a shot in the small hotel room. The man didn't hear it, being preoccupied with blinding pain. His knees fell away and he crashed again to the floor.

Lion knelt next to him—"Very rude"—and slammed his head onto the threadbare carpet.

The man coughed and hacked at his bloody nose and tried to pull himself away from the carpet threads stuck to his face.

"You is a sick fuck," Lion said, somewhere above him. "What you need is a cure."

The man had gotten up to his knees and was panting and snorting blood. "Look you—" he started to say.

Lion grabbed him by the ear in a cool, controlled move and pulled him up onto the bed. "Shit looks like shit, shit smells, shit don't talk!"

The man was lost for a moment in the bedclothes, his eyes dazzled with sheet, blanket...and his pain. When he had rolled enough he looked up, blinking, at Lion's cock.

The man was, indeed, a giant.

"Please," the man said.

Lion's laugh was as big as he was. It started down somewhere in his basement and boiled out of him in a shake that rattled the room's cheap prints like a train passing—or so it seemed to the man cowering on the bed.

The huge black man reached long and strong for the man's hair. With a single clench, Lion got almost all of it, then pulled the man toward him.

"First, you gotta clean it. And clean it good."

Lion's cock was beautiful and uncut. There was much talk of Lion's prowess among his rivals, enemies, and business acquaintances, and, surprisingly, they all pretty much agreed. Lion's cock was as muscled and as well-defined as his arm and, seemingly to the freak, as big. Veins ran over it like burls in a tree limb. His head, hidden by foreskin, was as big as a lightbulb.

Keeping his hand on the man, Lion reached down and pulled his foreskin back.

Precome dotted the sculpted tip of Lion's cock head like a pearl ring in a black silk jewelry case, shining white on the smooth black skin. Lion's cock head was fat and as strong as the rest of him.

"Clean me, shit," Lion said, readying another devastating slap in case he should resist.

Hardly. He kissed and then swallowed Lion's cock head like he was enjoying candy—a jawbreaker, considering Lion's size.

Despite himself, Lion found his grip on the back of the freak's head relaxing under his oral ministrations. There was cock sucking, Lion knew from the biz and his own peccadilloes, and then there was *cock sucking*. There was the variety of actions (like licking, sucking hard, tonguing, gentle chewing, tip probing, the whole menagerie), and then were the actions of the pure cocksucker. The guy, the man in room 414, was one born and true. Lion's cock was all this guy was focused on, all he existed for. His eyes were closed and he mewed, gentle and soft, like a kitten.

Lion was enjoying it. Rarely had he had a suck of this dedication—and it was Lion's point of pride that his stable of girls were all personally auditioned to assure quality. The freak in room 414 could have been prime property, if he wasn't shit.

But he *was* shit.

Lion pulled up, hard on his hair. Shocked, the freak almost bit but his deep down primal urge to not injure the lovely cock he was sucking kept his teeth apart.

Lion smiled and pulled the man up until they were face-to-face. "Shit *sucks*." Maybe there was a smile in Lion's voice, maybe humor, or maybe there wasn't. Hard to tell. If there was, then it wasn't enough to stop Lion from slapping the man again.

It sounded like someone had dropped a steak on the floor, a raw, fresh slice—still bleeding. With his other hand, Lion grabbed the man's thick brown leather belt and snapped it off. Then he grabbed the waist of the freak's pants and yanked down, hard.

Squirming, the man tried to kick and fight, but Lion held him like a crane above the bed. He tried to knee the giant black man in the chest and head, but all he seemed to do was glance off Lion's suit. The few blows he aimed at Lion's iron rod, the slick pole that felt like black rubber around a tire iron, didn't even make the black man blink.

The pants came off in three hard jerks that heated the man's knees from the abrading seersucker. A huge mitt grabbed the band of his BVDs—then they too were gone: to join the pile on the floor.

"You is sick," Lion said, holding the man up again so he had a direct and uninterrupted view of Lion's ivory and golds. "You is diseased, shit. You have to be sick in the head to do to what you did. Don't you like simple pleasures, shit? Don't you like it the way others do?"

The man tried to kick and scramble away. Lion's grip was tighter, stronger than handcuffs.

"You need the cure, shit."

With a flick of his wrist, Lion spun the man around. When he tried to scramble away, Lion held him on the bed with one hand on his ankle.

"You need the cure, bad," the pimp said, reaching under the freak and lifting him up. Then he spat on his asshole.

Lion was bigger going in than he was going down. The man screamed high and shrill, almost not a sound, as Lion pushed himself slowly, relentlessly into him. Above him, Lion laughed again—jungle drums—at the scream. Inches felt like feet. Lion leaned forward for better purchase.

The insertion, for the freak, was like a boxcar coasting through the yards: slow but unstoppable. He could feel himself tear even as he tried to relax against the filling pressure. He grunted to release the cramping in his belly, trying to sound out the pain of the entry. He tried to crawl away from Lion's cock in his asshole, but the pimp's grip was an iron cuff.

Somewhere distant from where the freak was having rolling stock pushing into him, something tickled the cheeks of his ass.

It felt like two blackjacks knocking against him—blackjacks covered in coarse horsehair.

Lion's balls, he realized, distantly of course.

The pimp fucked him hard. His rhythm wasn't fast; it was relentless—a slamming drumbeat that got heavier and heavier. Slick, wet slapping—and the man's grunts—filled the room. Lion started to shine, like someone had given his fine mahogany a polish. Lion had his mouth slightly open, and breathed heavy past his ivory and gold teeth like a train leaving on a long haul.

Each stroke ended with filling pain, ended with Lion's thick black cock ramming deeper and deeper into the freak's asshole. It knocked his kidneys around and the man felt himself ache to piss. It slammed his guts and seemed to knock against his heart, a jazz mix to his regular pounding pulse.

Lion reached down and grabbed the man's hair again, getting a good grip of his brown locks, and pulled up, hard.

The man's groan boiled out of him as Lion impaled him back against the full, full depth of his cock.

Lion growled deep Africa—his namesake calling across the veldt—and turned to black stone. Stiff, hard, he stood there for four quick beats of the freak's heart.

Somewhere, somewhere inside him, the man felt himself fill with Lion's come. He felt Lion's cock twitch and jerk as it kicked white juice into him.

Then Lion threw him away. The bed was soft and he almost bounced off it to fall against the window, but he caught the bedclothes and stopped himself with a floral anchor.

Lion stood on the other side of the bed, gleaming with sweat where his black skin showed around his fine suit. Then slowly, as patiently as the action of a fine timepiece, he folded away his thick black cock and zipped his fly. "You's cured now, shit. You cured of what ailed you. You done taken a rightly big dose of

Lion's medicine." He went to the door, but stopped and turned. "You do what you did again, shit, and I'm gonna have to operate." Then Lion left, closing the door slowly and certainly.

Maxine didn't like Darrin drinking mint juleps, he said in his Tennessee twang that his regulars loved to hear him talk filth with, because it made him look like a queer.

"I hate to disappoint you," Darrin said, throwing his hair back in a classical debutante's swish, "but looks do tell."

Then Darrin saw someone come through the green-tinted crystal doors of the 87 Club. "Run along now, sweetie," he said, dismissing Maxine with a wave of his hand, "I have business to conduct."

After Maxine had left, with a pouting, stinging retort, Darrin pulled a chair out for his guest, who sat down gingerly, as if he'd been kicked by a horse.

"No disappointments?" Darrin said, sipping his drink and batting his eyes.

Room 414 nodded, smiling, and took a thick wad of bills out of his pocket and slid it across the marble tabletop to Darrin. "Perfect," he said.

Darrin made the bills disappear. "Thank God," he said with a theatrical sigh as he dipped an 87 Club napkin in his drink and wiped the rest of the "blood" from his face. "I was starting to attract the wrong type of clientele."

"It was all you promised," the man said. "Thank you." And then he left.

As he did, as the man parted the doors of the 87 Club and walked out onto Bourbon Street, Darrin said, "Good for what ails you," and sipped his drink.

Wet

The brush was dry so he wet it.

Doud never really thought of changing mediums for his work. Never really thought about changing to, say, oils or watercolors. He knew them, had touched them here or there. But always he'd come back to the pure wet.

Always the bold, straight streaks: vertical, horizontal, diagonal. The same start. The canvas soon a blur of dark and light reds, maybe a form there, maybe not. A foggy world seen by the light of a dying fire.

The brush was dry. *Dries so quickly.* Calmly, he dipped it and fell back into the painting. Maybe a man. Yes, perhaps that. A fuzzy blotch becoming a head, a soft smudge becoming shoulders. The movements of the brush were wild, feverish. Dry again.

Doud dipped the brush into his red-filled mouth and tried to capture the man more fully. The image grew like leaves from a tree: the curves of a chest, tendons in the arms, the contours of muscle and bone, a face.... Precise strokes skittered and scratched across the smooth face of the canvas.

The brush was dry so he wet it.

The street was brilliant with a heaven of shines and reflections from a light rain. The primary neon colors bursting from places like Jackson's Hole, the Ten Pin, the 87 Club, Aunt Mary's Diner hit the street, the sidewalk, the faces of the tall buildings like...*watercolors*, Doud thought. His own medium was a lot less flowing and fluid.

The Space didn't have neon. Its owner, Wellington, would never even ponder lighting its very nondescript doorway with such a gaudy attraction. Wellington took extremely cool pride in the austerity of his gallery—going over its rubber-tiled steps, eggshell walls, industrial lighting, stainless steel display stands, and single office countertop with an eye as precise and chilly as a level. Doud easily imagined him thinking the photographs, paintings, and sculptures that paid his rent a distraction from the purity of an absolutely empty room.

Doud hoped for a frozen second that the flash had been lightning beyond the window, out among the glimmering night street and its hunched and brisk people. He loved the rain and especially lightning. As with the bands of slow, precise color that started his works, he never really examined why the world being lit for a second, frozen and trapped in a blink of pure silver, fascinated him. Maybe it was the raw power of natural electricity, or maybe it was the comfort of being snug and warm with rain outside: Lightning was the tiger prowling outside while he warmed his feet, safe and warm, inside.

But it wasn't lightning. It was photography.

Trapped with the flash was his own face: wide, large brown eyes; aquiline nose; brushy brows; curled black hair; deeply

tanned, lined skin; large, strong mouth with hidden teeth. Some
thought him Italian, others American or East Indian. A few
guessed at maybe Eskimo or even Polynesian. Never guessed the
truth. Never, ever, guessed his age.

The disappointment over a lightning-free night came quick,
a gentle slap (because it was a simple pleasure) and he turned
back to the semicrowded gallery. Doud spotted him: a too-clean
photographer he instantly pegged as either the friend of an artist
or an artist himself. (Newspaper shooters were usually a lot more
scruffy and exotic.) Doud hated to be photographed, hated being
frozen in time and having his image in the hands of, at the mercy
of, someone else.

"Yours?" the photographer said, his face opaqued by the complex of a flash unit, massive lens, and a matte-black camera body.
Dirty blond, almost brown, tall, broad—was all Doud could see.

"Those are," Doud said, nodding to the right-hand wall and
the five paintings. Doud didn't need to see them, an artist's privilege of many hours of work.

The camera came down and the photographer treated Doud
to his profile as he scanned the paintings: pale, hollow cheeks;
bones seemingly as thin as a bird's; wet blue eyes that, even across
the mostly empty gallery, seemed to see far too much, far too
quickly; a mouth that bloomed with lips Doud instantly wanted
to kiss; a nose all but invisible against the beauty of his face; and
a fine and elegant body that seemed to be all chest and shoulders,
a rack on which thin, pale arms and legs dangled with a dignified
posture. He was dressed simply in black pants, a very tight turtle-
neck, and an antique morning coat—a direct polar extreme from
Doud's old sweatshirt, boots, and jeans.

It was a kind of shock to see someone so...dapper—a word
that came out of Doud's memory along with the smell of horses and raw electricity, the rumble of the "El" trains, and

scratchy Al Jolson from a Gramophone. Dapper? Yes, refined and polished. Quite out of character for The Space and an admirer of Doud's work.

"You probably get asked this a lot—" the man started to say, fixing his darting eyes on Doud and smiling pure warmth.

"An awful lot," Doud said with a practiced sigh that spoke of a joke rather than true exasperation. "Animals," he finished, answering the question.

"I saw the jar," the photographer said, indicating with a jerk of his camera the large bell jar stuffed with a cow's severed head on the floor in front of Doud's wall, "and thought as much."

"The medium is the message," Doud said with a smile. "People either look at me *real* funny and think about DNA testing, or they think it's a trick of paint and technique. I put out the cow's head so they know."

"It's rather...your studio must really stink."

Doud laughed, the sound coming from down deep, "Lots of windows, and I keep my stuff well-covered. Then I seal it after. Lots of shellac."

The man smiled, shifted his camera, and stuck out a pale, long-boned hand. "Jona. Jona Periliak."

"Charmed," Doud said. Jona's hand was dry and very warm, almost hot. "Are you here as well, or just taking shots for a friend?"

"I'm in the back room."

Doud remembered the photographs, but since he never supervised his installations he hadn't looked beyond that initial glance. "Would you mind," Doud said, smiling his best smile and hoping he'd remembered to gargle and brush his teeth, "showing me?"

The Space had really started to fill up since they'd been talking. The usual wine-and-cheese crowd of artists and their usual mixture of friends. They passed carefully by suits and jeans and piercings and Doc Martens and even a latex bodysuit and a full tuxedo.

The back room was sky-blue, lit with Wellington's usual baby spots. Maybe a dozen, maybe 14 black-and-white self-portraits. Jona looking thoughtful with glasses and a book. Jona looking sad with gravestones in the background. Jona looking pained as blood, black as ink (and it could have been), ran down from a sliced palm. Jona excited, his bare chest slick with sweat and probably oil. Doud scanned them, lingering long over excited and pained, then glanced at the title of the series: "Portrait of the Artists."

"They're fine," Doud said. He didn't like photographs for lots of reasons, but Jona was very pretty, very striking in his pallor and funereal garb. Self-portraits made it easy to lie—Jona was very fine, indeed.

"You don't like them." Jona didn't seem hurt at all, more like he was calling Doud on his politeness.

"I didn't say that. It's not my medium is all. Besides, I meant what I said. They're fine. I like the way these are all parts of you."

"I can appreciate that," Jona said, moving the camera behind him so Doud had a nice view of his flat stomach and hard chest.

It had been a long time for Doud. He could barely remember the face, and couldn't, for the life of him, think of the last name of the last person he was attracted to as much as he was attracted to Jona. *You'd think*, he found himself thinking with surprising clarity, *after all this time I'd get better at this.*

At least he wasn't hungry—but he did feel that other kind of desperation, the one that wanted to make his gently shaking hands reach up and stroke Jona's soft, pale cheeks and tell him how beautiful he looked. *Go on*, he thought next, *say that you want him.*

"Are you," Doud did say, waving at the row of photographs, "going to be here long?"

"Tonight or the show?" And before Doud could respond either way, Jona added, "Just a few minutes and the end of the month."

The Space had filled up, and Doud felt himself being pulled by the crowd's body heat, their eyes. Going to an opening was rare, staying as late as he had was ever rarer, but Jona, and Jona's beautiful attention, was priceless. But the people...

"It's kind of getting crowded," the pale beauty said with a smile that made a warm spot on Doud's stomach and his eyes lose focus for a second.

Doud heard himself say, "Let's go outside."

Doud liked the ships and the trains. And the rent was cheap. He could understand why others didn't like living next to the yards, in front of the bay, especially when one of the big diesel engines revved at 1 A.M. or a tramp steamer blasted its departure at 2.

Despite being jerked awake too damned early in the morning, Doud liked living in the shadow of the simple, huge machines. People made him feel alone and way too unique, outside always looking in and...hungry. The boats and the trains made him feel practically human by comparison.

"You never said why you didn't like my shots," Jona said, sitting on Doud's comfortable burgundy sofa, twirling a quarter-full glass of white wine.

"I guess I think it's a cheat."

"That it takes a lot less to handle a camera than a brush?"

"Not necessarily," Jona said, leaning forward to look into Doud's eyes.

Doud looked so quickly away it made his head hurt for a moment. "You never asked why I paint the way I do," he said to his spiraling red and blue rug.

"I thought it had something to do with the cycle of death. You know, something growing from something dying. Your pictures from dead cows."

Doud found himself frowning: another person who didn't pick up on it. He wondered why he had any kind of following at all, or was it just that people liked seeing paintings done in blood? "No," he said, refilling his glass even though he knew he'd had way too much already. "That's not really it. I do it to give them something close to immortality."

Jona was rapt. In many ways more rapt than he should have been. "But you don't like photographs."

Doud sighed, hated saying these kinds of things but also tired of lying. Yeah, lying usually got him company for the night, or even a weekend, but he didn't like how he felt in the morning, on Monday. At least when he told the truth he liked the company that stuck around. "Nothing lasts forever," he finally said after a long damned silence. (God, Jona was pretty.) "Except for a photograph. Throw the negative away, then maybe a print will age and fade away naturally. Won't last absolutely forever. I paint because the...animals will last so much longer. Not forever. Just a lot, lot longer."

Jona smiled and sipped his wine. "You don't like forever?"

Doud shook his head, slow and tired: the sound of iron wheels on cobblestones, opium, a harbor full of sails, coal... "Nothing ever is. A long, long time...yes. But not forever. Nothing is ever forever."

Jona thought for a long time, twirling the wine in his glass in what Doud decided could be a very annoying habit. Then he put the glass down carefully on Doud's spiraling rug and dug in a cotton shoulder bag he had brought from The Space. He came up with a stiff manila envelope, and, never once meeting Doud's eyes, undid the clasp and removed a sandwich of gray cardboard. Between them: a city street in a copy of plate sepia; carriage bus filigreed with advertisements for patent medicines and Clothiers for Fine, Respected Gentlemen; women in hoop skirts, men with top hats and swallow-tailed coats; children in sailor suits, pinafores, and button-up shoes; a man in a wool coat and a simple bowler, with a casual, caught-unawares face—handsome eagle nose, dark features that could be Italian, Mediterranean, East Indian....

I hate photographs, Doud thought hollowly, coldly.

Jona sat in a little coffeehouse, the Kona Coast, and kept the words circulating in his mind, trying to keep them fresh, trying not to lose a scrap.

His lips and throat hurt. Getting up that morning, he'd coughed a fat, dark slug of phlegm and blood into Doud's bathroom sink. By noon his lips were a faded purple and it hurt to smile.

Kona Coast wasn't his first choice, something less loaded would have been much better. But he didn't seem to have any room in his mind to think of someplace new, original: Jeffrey's favorite place would have to do.

It's painful till you get used to it. Let your body acclimate to its new design.

He felt good. Damned good. The world was sharp and clean and crisp. Looking across the tiny coffeehouse he felt his attention glide like a scalpel across the wooden tables, the stacks of free newspapers, the walls decorated years thick with roommate wanted, jobs offered, bands playing, films showing fliers and handbills. Someone walked in and for a second, not even a heart-beat, he thought it was Jeffrey. But with his new focus, his new clean eyes, he saw that the face across the room was not even close. This man had gray at his temples. Jeffrey was too vain to allow even a single aging hair.

Am I the only one? I guess I might be. I've made...friends like you a few times. You get lonely, and it's hard to get close to your food—at least emotionally. I don't know if they've managed to make...friends like I can. I don't think they can.
I don't know if I'm a myth or a fluke. I was born this way.

Looking down in his coffee, Jona caught and captured the wisps of steam, freezing them with his mind as the words of Doud echoed around the chitchat of the coffeehouse. At first he was too excited, and in too much pain, to hear it clearly. But there, in the Kona Coast, he and Doud were there, moving in front of him like the steam from his white and sweet coffee.

Two things. Remember the two things of what you are now. I give you one but not the other: Murder. Immortality.

Again, Jeffrey intruded on Jona's recollection of Doud: Jeffrey standing in front of him again. Another fight. Another argument. Jona's shock and outrage over something Jona had said or done. That outrage—it made Jona furious. Jeffrey's blank, shocked look, his wet eyes, as he tried to understand why Jona had done what he'd done. Didn't matter what he'd done—said something catty, made some remark, flirted with someone's partner, fucked someone's partner, stolen some useless knickknack—there was

Jeffrey's smug, shining face whipping Jona with just a disappointed look. He hated Jeffrey when he looked at him like that. Hated his boring superiority.

Like I said, I don't know what I am. Many things, labels, work, but mostly they don't. Sunlight doesn't hurt, crosses don't do anything. Stakes will—but then they'll probably kill anything. I have to eat twice, sometimes only once, if I take it easy, every six months. I can do more, but don't.

The photograph of Doud. Jona remembered where he'd gotten it with an electric flash. Some friend of Jeffrey's, a smug little queen with an arrogant love of and dedication to antiques. The little shit was too in love with his partner, an ebony beauty named Tan, to respond to Jona's come-on, so he'd compensated by lifting an album of turn-of-the-century photographs.

Jeffrey had found out, of course, and had shown up at Jona's little Park Circle studio to demand the book back.

Seeing his ex-lover standing in his front room and looking down at him like dirt, Jona had quaked with anger. "Do you see it here?" he'd said, trying not to betray his fury.

"I know you took it, Jo." Jeffrey had said.

"If you can find it, then call me a fucking thief. If you don't see it, then get the fuck out."

Jeffrey'd never looked, just left saying he didn't want to know Jona anymore.

After Doud had done...whatever it was he'd had done, he had put Jona, heaving, panting, and vibrating like a junkie, on his coach, dried and not-dried blood like paste all over his face and chest and mouth. Doud had been crying, almost puking with the tears dribbling from his large eyes: "I'm so sorry. So sorry. I just want some company. It's stupid. I'm so stupid. I don't know you. Don't know you at all..."

In one of the photographs he recognized a man from an upcoming installation at The Space. The medium and the perfect likeness: He didn't really think anything about it, didn't really put anything together about it aside from another game, another trick. Show Doud the shot, freak him the fuck out, and pick up the pieces as he'd done so many times before. Just another game.

With Jeffrey it had been fucking anything that moved—easy because Jeffrey liked to *bond* with his lovers. Easy to dick with someone who just wants *you*—you fuck someone else.

"You have to, but you don't have to enjoy it. I do it. I do it but I try to atone as best I can. I make it quick, I don't enjoy it. I don't do it for any other reason than to survive. And...yes, I try to make it up to them somehow: make them special. Give them a long, long life. Almost immortality."

The doors to the little coffeehouse opened again, and Jona's steam, and Doud's words in his mind, vanished in the cool breeze. Glancing up, he saw with his new, crystal eyes a tall, slender man sporting shoulder-length brown curls without a trace of gray.

"Jeffrey," Jona said to him, motioning Jeffrey to the table.

"What do you want, Jona?" Jeffrey said, walking over but standing stiff and straight.

"I have something to tell you," Jona said.

"Is it about Abbott's book? If you have it, you should get it back to him. I don't want to see it, know about it, or have anything to do with you."

"Jeffrey," Jona said, with a spark of playful warmth in his voice, "don't you think you owe me at least a little chance, a tiny one, to end this well? I don't want you to hate me, Jeffrey."

"Is it the book, Jona?" It was rare to see Jeffrey almost angry. Fury crashed through Jona like a metal wave and he tasted copper in his mouth and on his bruised and swollen lips.

But then Jona firmly recalled Doud, the kiss, the new self in him, the new world he was about to walk into, and so he said, smiling despite his very painful lips, "Yes, Jeffrey, it's the book. But much more. Come back to my place and I'll tell you all about it."

Jona had slept the night before, his face and mouth wet with blood, in Doud's bed. As the sun started to burn up the city he had gotten cleaned up and gone straight to the Kona Coast for thought and coffee. Then Jeffrey.

Though Jeffrey was a few inches taller than gaunt and hallow-cheeked Jona, he seemed smaller somehow, as if the night, Doud, and the blood, had added to him. A lot.

Jeffrey tagged along as Jeffrey always did, a few steps behind, scanning the dim and damp streets from the coffeehouse to Jona's place. They didn't talk much, the silence between them a hard wall of skewed viewpoints. Jeffrey felt betrayed by Jona, deceived and manipulated too many times.

Jona looked back over his shoulder. His viewpoint was...simpler: *I like looking down on you, Jeffrey. There is so little to you, really. So very little. Just like everyone else. So very little.*

"I don't really want to come up," Jeffrey said, standing on the slick marble of the foyer as Jona clinked and rattled his keys.

"But you want the book, don't you?" Jona said, opening the door and stepping aside.

"I want closure," Jeffrey said, shouldering past and starting up the two flights to Jona's apartment.

"Well, so do I," Jona said, from behind him, as he closed the door.

Another rattle of keys, another door. Again Jeffrey stepped in first, scanning the apartment slowly even though nothing had changed since he'd last been there. Closing the door behind him, Jona smiled wide and broad against the thud of pain from his lips. The smile had sprung from a giddy relief that he could see Jeffrey clearly, very clearly, for the first time.

So little to you, Jeffrey. So damned little. And to think I envied you, your grace and meticulous gestures. Your subtle humor. Your gliding hands. I loved to make you...all of you, do what I wanted. Cry. Laugh. Get so frustrated. Now I don't need to.

Now I'm much more.

"Can I have a kiss, Jeffrey?" Jona said softly, trying to hide the laughter that wanted to explode out of him as he put a careful, gentle hand on Jeffrey's high shoulder.

"Jona," Jeffrey said, struck suddenly sad by the tone in Jona's voice.

"I just want something to close all this. A kiss would be perfect. Perfect. Then the photographs. I promise."

"Always playing fucking games." Jeffrey's voice was level and smooth, crisp and elegant as always. But Jona knew he was furious, that he shook with anger beneath his cultivated image. "No more hoops, Jona. You're not in love with me. You never were. You're not anything you pretended to be. I saw you, Jona. I saw you when you dicked us all around and played with my head. When you fucked around. Smiling. Always fucking smiling."

"So I don't even deserve a good-bye kiss?" Jona said, trying desperately not to smile.

Doud stood in a short alley reeking of vomit and urine and

watched the shadows moving against a hard light. The rain was cold, and, of course, wet, but his concentration on the one window dimmed it down to the gentle stings of the drops in his eyes. He didn't blink. Didn't need to. He could now find Jona anywhere in the city: There were other things he could do, but frankly, he rarely had a need for them.

How many times? Doud thought, looking down at the sparkling streets for a second, listening to the hushed passing of cars, moving through a night frozen at moments with lightning flashes. *How many times have I stood like this and waited? How many times have I stood and watched, knowing I'd be alone again in a few hours?*

But there was hope in the back of his mind, a glow, the same little glow that always accompanied those other thoughts: *Maybe just this once.*

The heat from Jeffrey was an open flame in Jona's face. Jona was normally a blackout kisser, letting his eyes squeeze shut with the concentration of a good kiss, rolling in the play of tongue and lips and teeth. But his eyes were wide open now—wide and capturing Jeffrey as he bent down the few inches to kiss him, catching the tiny pores on the end of what he'd always thought of as a perfect nose. He saw the tiny broken blood vessels in Jeffrey's eyes, the silken bags under those eyes that would worsen with age; caught a hint of wine and garlic on Jeffrey's breath that meant tall, elegant Jeffrey had been haunting his goth friends for company. Jona took him in with a glance and a breath in the moment Jeffrey relaxed to kiss. Jona saw bone and sweat and piss and shit and muscle and guts and the raging, boiling inferno of quarts and quarts of blood. Jona didn't see, for once, the statue that had deemed Jona good in bed and worthy of his debonair company.

Jona's cock was iron, steel in his pants. He wanted to reach down and stroke it, rub himself to a nice orgasm as he held himself high above the simple meat of the man he'd thought of as perfect, idolized. He wanted to orgasm from just standing there—the ego rush of realizing what Jeffrey really was and what Jona was now. His cock raged full and hard, straining with the pure power of being someone else at last, at being powerful at last.

Kiss me.

The touch was a shock. Jona was so focused, so drawn into his perception of the puppet, the hunk of gristle that was Jeffrey, that he didn't expect the touch to be silken and sparked with tension. He jerked back a tiny amount, breaking the contact as quickly as it had been made. He expected something rough and coarse to match his meaty revelation about his old flame.

Then he moved closer.

The touch was softer this time, and the two old lovers fell into the comfort of each other's bodies. Jeffrey might have wanted something chaste and simple, a gothic rite of departure like a Victorian greeting card—"Nice to have known your acquaintance"—but the jungle fury that suddenly flickered out of Jona washed the practiced distance right out of him.

It was a good kiss. A fine kiss. It was a lover's kiss at the height of their attraction.

It didn't seem like a kiss good-bye.

As Jona started, Jeffrey's cock went from a strong erection to a painful hardness in his precise pants. It was the first indication that Jona had started it right. He was surprised over how natural, how easy it felt, like the comfort of...a lover's kiss. Jona just followed the way that seemed right and it flowed along with the simple determination of any biological function. Like kissing, like drinking, like swallowing, like eating.

Like breathing. Jona kissed Jeffrey and started to breathe him in. Gently at first, but then stronger and stronger. Jeffrey liked it, liked the strong suction of Jona's mouth on his, liked the earthy pull of his lungs on his own.

Then he tasted blood and his chest started to hurt.

The kiss climbed from the edge-hard passion of rough sex, of their cocks pressing—dueling clubs between their frenzied bodies. It went from that flash of painful sex to pure pain to screaming.

But Jeffrey couldn't scream. Jona's mouth was over his and he was pulling Jeffrey inside out through his own throat.

Jona felt Jeffrey's pure, hot blood boil up and out and down his throat. He pulled and tugged with his breath and the other of his new self. Jona reached down with his hunger and pulled Jeffrey out of himself. The blood and essence was a scalding wine of life splashing against his lips, teeth, gums, and tongue. He wanted to laugh, to scream his joy and power to the moon, to the sun. But more than that, more than anything he wanted *more*. He wanted the totality of the meat and blood (oh, yes, the *blood*) of Jeffrey. He wanted to drink him to the last drop, to pull him all the way in, to drink him through their kiss until there was nothing more to hold, to stroke—until Jeffrey's threatening perfection was nothing but a slaughterhouse residue.

Jona's cock was iron, something fundamental and material in the torrent of life he was pulling out of Jeffrey. He wanted to fuck something, anything. He wanted to drive his spur of metal into a worthy, powerful lover.

He thought of Doud. He thought of the little man in the jeans and the sweater. Doud had stopped, had held back just enough of Jona, and then had forced the blood, water, tears, come, meat back into him. He'd tasted Jona, and put him back into his now changed body.

He could do the same, he guessed, with Jeffrey—but he didn't want to. Didn't want to at all. He was hungry and thirsty and Jeffrey just...tasted too damned good.

In his arms, Jeffrey screamed into his mouth and diminished in stature. Jona pulled the fluids out of him, drew the essence and blood out of him and down his own throat. Hypnotized, Jona watched Jeffrey's skin darken and lose its shine; saw blindness glaze Jeffrey's eyes; saw Jeffrey's cheeks concave and his bones snap from the pressure, the spreading dryness.

Soon—*too soon!*—Jona held the child-size husk of Jeffrey, a dusty bag of whining, chalk-soft bones and papery skin. Still he pulled and pulled. Jeffrey snapped and tore and crackled like a low fire or paper being crumpled. The last drop of wet tasted of music: a single high note that passed his teeth and dropped like a bell into Jona's stomach, body.

There was little left of elegant Jeffrey: an ancient doll of hair, scraps of skin, fingernails, and shattered bones like dice in a bag. Not enough to identify—easily buried or flushed down the toilet.

Jona put the dry fragments of Jeffrey on the floor and stretched, feeling the blood surge and roll in his strong body, feeling it mix and burn with his own. He felt exalted, added to, charged...

Full.

Jeffrey rolled in the back of Jona's throat, a warm wine filling him, draining into him. Jona caught a steaming reflection in one of the windows and laughed at himself. *Friends sometimes leave an impression on you*, he thought to his normal, slender reflection. *Jeffrey, I guess, didn't on me.*

Doud was watching an engine back into the yards when his doorbell rang. He'd known it would soon enough, but it happened faster than he'd expected.

Going to the door, he checked to make sure his hat, coat, and shoes weren't anywhere in sight. His *wet* hat, coat, and shoes.

"Come in," he said to a dripping Jona. "I've missed you."

"I like that," Jona said, entering and shaking water from his coat before handing it to Doud, "People don't usually miss me."

"I did. I've missed you for a long time. Longer than today, even."

"Been a long time?" Jona said from the front room, looking back at Doud hanging up his coat, the words sinking into him. "I guess it has."

"Very long. It's hard to relate to others. You should find that out quickly. It's just the two of us."

"Intimate," Jona said, sitting on the couch. "I like intimate. Just the two of us against the world."

"The world would win. Drink?"

"Sure."

As Doud rattled and banged in the kitchen, Jona called: "How long, Doud?"

"What do you mean?"

"I mean, how long?"

"No, I mean how long for what? How long since I was this way? Forever. I told you: born this way. Since I got laid? A month ago this Thursday, in the afternoon. Since I've had real...companionship? Twenty years, give or take. Since I killed someone for food? Seven months."

"Do you like this, Doud?" Jona said from the door to the kitchen. There was something in his voice; in the tones, if not the words. It wasn't a deep ponder or a frightened seek for answers. Not laughter, not excitement—nothing so obvious. Not even a smile.

Close, though. Close to a smile.

"I don't have a choice. You have a cut cock, Jona—do you like that? Does it matter? I have always been this way. Always. I don't know what people are really like, all those people out there. I just know what I am, and what I have had to do to live...for as long as I have."

"But you're not one of them."

"I'm something. Something that needs to suck 'em bone-dry to survive. So I have to keep myself distant from them," Doud said, handing Jona a simple white wine in a cheap glass. "Can't have cows as friends, you know."

"Is that how you really see them?"

"No. I don't. But they're not what I am. I miss someone I can talk to, share my life with. Be with when the 'otherness' is everywhere. I do what I have to do to keep living, but that's all. It's enough, though, to keep them out there and me in here."

"Well," Jona said, knocking back half of his glass with one swallow, "it's not you anymore. It's us."

Doud smiled soft, small, and quick, saying, "I appreciate that. I do."

"I appreciate you, Doud: what you've given me."

"It...almost makes it worthwhile, to be able to see people grow up. Buggies to Neil Armstrong. Typhus and children's bars to Apple and the Web."

Smiling, Jona sat next to Doud on the couch. "I'm looking forward to it. I'm really..." *smiling* "...looking forward to it."

"I'm glad you are," Doud said. "I'm glad."

Time dragged as they sipped their wine. As it often happens, their heat was a magnet. First they sat in uncomfortable, hard, silence. Then they were closer, touching cotton pants to jeans. The temperature for both was clearly higher. Doud's hand ended up on Jona's knee. Thinking about it later, Doud thought that he probably (since he usually did) was talking, maintaining an empty patter of god-knew what: stories of elevated trains, shooting the moon, coonskin coats, outdoor plumbing, *The Yellow Kid*, short pants, a woman's well-turned ankle—a smoke screen of articulated memories hiding his fear of the temperature between them.

Finally Jona leaned over and kissed him.

Doud's patter vanished into a low, purring moan—one that made Jona smile a painful smile in the middle of the kiss.

When they broke, Doud smiled too. He reached out and put a hand on Jona's hard cock, stroking it lightly, ghostly, through Jona's jeans. "No secrets, none at all."

"Wouldn't have it any other way," Jona said, stretching, leaning back until he was a length of crackling joints.

Doud's hands were almost shaking as he undid Jona's fly, pulled his pants away from his waist, revealing softly pale skin—no underwear—and hints of distant, scratchy, hairs.

Jona lifted his ass off the couch and Doud fought and struggled with Jona's jeans until they surrendered and jerked down his firm thighs.

Jona's cock wasn't huge. No exaggerations: It was simply average. A pale column of very hard meat, head a brilliant pink. Cut. Noticeably fatter at the root than the tip, despite a wide corona. It bobbed, a gentle swaying, with a creamy drop of early excitement gleaming at the tip.

"Beautiful," Doud said, wrapping his lips around Jona's cock.

It was like a pressurized bath to Jona, a silken, damp hand strong around the nerves of his cock. A quiet man, a gothic gentleman of the night, Jona actually made a sound. As Doud kissed the tip, then licked the shaft, then dropped his warm, wet mouth over Jona's entire cock, Jona made a soft, all-but-inaudible, mewing sound.

It was hard for him not to instantly come.

Practice, Jona thought. Lots and lots of practice. Years of practice.

Doud's mouth was more than well-trained. It was magical. Jona felt a tongue as nimble as fingers, as strong as an ass, as precise as an eyelash. He was lost completely to Doud's tongue, teeth, palate, lips, and warm saliva. It was hard for him to focus on anything save the tiny, incredible details of Doud's lips and mouth on him.

Somewhere deep inside the raging sea of Doud's expert cock sucking, a little Jona was smiling and leaning back, sketching the territory of the future in his mind, playing the angles, and seeing where he might take it. *Simple, Doud. Very simple, Doud. What's yours now will be mine later: with enough time. Now I have lots of time for lots of things...lots of fun things.*

In there, in his thoughts, he tripped over the corpse of Jeffrey, sticks and stones in a bag of dried, vanishing skin. It was a quiet moment, remembering Jeffrey's eyes crumbling back into their sockets, his last scream vanishing into crackling bones, tearing skin.

Then he came.

It was a screaming come, a deep brass come—all horns and woodwinds. A primal orgasm that pushed, heaved, and kicked its way from the base of his balls up through his cock and out the top, mixing and splashing in Doud's mouth and even foaming his dark lips.

Laughing, Jona leaned forward and mussed Doud's thick, curly hair. "That was—"

"Not yet," Doud said, his voice unreadable as he licked the come from Jona's still-hard cock. "Not yet."

Doud set back to work, performing his mouthy magic on Jona again. And again Jona was on a road to a shaking, squirming come—a fast trip straight down, no bends, pedal to the floor. The persistence of Doud was almost frightening, almost made Jona open his eyes wide. It was so good—too good. It was frightening. It was as if Doud had plugged himself directly into Jona's cock, had thrown a switch to make him come and come and come.

He did and did and did.

It didn't stop. One come after another, each squirt a little less than the one before, each a little less good and a little more...forced. Each one more of a strain.

Then the pain started.

Jona tried to make Doud stop but the pain was too much. It was all he could do to hang on to the couch and let the hot iron being poured down his cock come out as a deep, echoing scream. His balls felt like they were cracking, breaking apart from the pressure of Doud's suction. His cock was tearing, it was ripping from the inside out from the force of Doud's lips, the strength of his body reaching into Jona and pulling him out through his cock. Again and again he tried to move, to make his spasming, cramping hands let loose of the couch and bring them down on Doud to make him stop, but the cramps were like handcuffs around his wrists, wrapped around his fingers, trapping him there.

Then Doud stopped and said, blood and come dripping down his chin, eyes lit with fire from inside, "I promised you near forever—not a weapon, not a toy for you to enjoy. I gave you years, not murders."

Weak, Jona pushed himself off the couch, trying to speak, trying to get up and get away. But he was old, broken, and drained. Muscles in him, in his stomach, in his chest, were wrung tight and locked around broken bones. His cock was stuffed with needles and pins, his balls were crushed. Something dripped onto the floor and his cock was wet, very wet.

"You have blood on your lips," Doud said, wiping his mouth on his sleeve. Then he kissed Jona hard. Very hard. A kiss goodbye, like the kiss Jona had given Jeffrey.

Blood boiled up through the boiling arteries in Jona's throat. He felt them burst like blisters, felt the blood squirt and run. He felt his belly pull itself up under the power of Doud's kiss. He wanted to scream, wanted to cough and puke and cry, but he was just a straw, a tube for his own blood to travel through—out of his rupturing body and into Doud.

He tried to fight, to flail against the horrible pull of Doud, but his strength was laced with agony.

His eyesight fogged with blood. Then, with tearing agony, his eyeballs collapsed into themselves. Distantly, Jona felt his bones break, felt tearings and pullings deep within and surges of fluids—burning, sweet, sour—come up his throat, into his mouth, and into the vacuum of Doud.

Then all of him, all of him that was wet, did, completely, totally—and he was dead.

The brush was dry so he wet it.

Doud never really thought of changing mediums for his work. Never really thought about changing to, say, oils or watercolors. He knew them, had touched them here or there. But always he'd come back to the pure wet.

Always the bold, straight streaks: vertical, horizontal, diagonal. The same start. The canvas soon a blur of dark and light reds, maybe a form there, maybe not. A foggy world seen by the light of a dying fire.

The brush was dry. *Dries so quickly*. Calmly, he dipped it and fell back into the painting. Maybe a man. Yes, perhaps that. A fuzzy blotch becoming a head, a soft smudge becoming shoulders. The movements of the brush were wild, feverish. Dry again.

Doud dipped the brush into his red-filled mouth and tried to capture the man more fully. The image grew like leaves from a tree: the curves of a chest, tendons in the arms, the contours of muscle and bone, a face.... Precise strokes skittered and scratched across the smooth face of the canvas.

The brush was dry so he wet it.

Puppy

One morning Leo found a puppy asleep on his doorstep.

After stumbling into the warm and wiring embrace of his Peet's special Guatemalan blend with a flash of milk and a spoon of raw sugar and crawling into his work clothes, he'd noticed a sound somewhere between the whining of a keyhole saw and an electric drill countersinking wood screws. Leo poked his head out the window and craned to find the source. It was then that he discovered the whining young puppy.

Leo didn't consider himself a pet person. Still, there was something special about the Puppy. For one thing, it seemed to emit a glow of pure, 100-watt, innocence, as if it were a cross between a golden retriever and the archangel Gabriel. Its hair was sunlight–bright from the top of its head to the downy patch between its legs. The rest was as smooth and white as fine porcelain.

Seeing Leo, the Puppy ceased its lumberyard whine and stretched and yawned in the cutest way. The Puppy thought, *Well, are you gonna let me in or not?*

Naturally, it wasn't long before Leo opened his front door

and the Puppy bounded inside. The Puppy scampered to Leo and gave him a huge hug and a sweet, sloppy-wet kiss on the face before playfully jumping away and prancing at Leo's feet—yipping, chirping, barking like Leo was the Master come down from the Mount.

Leo, despite the rough, tough, bear image he liked to display, smiled a sparkling and wide smile, and let loose a barrel-rolling laugh that started at his size 12s, rumbled up his furry legs, echoed inside his massive and extraordinarily hairy chest, and escaped his bearded face and mustached lips. Leo actually, incredibly found himself thinking, *How cute. How fucking cute.*

"There, boy." Leo said, rubbing the Puppy on the top of its blond head and scratching behind its ears.

The Puppy responded with a round of fresh yips, yaps, and barks, and playfully butted and bit at Leo's overalls. Before Leo could stop it, the frisky beast had managed to bite and play at the overalls so much that they were suddenly around Leo's ankles.

"Hey!" Leo said, making a clumsy play for his clothes, all the time thinking, *My, aren't you playful?*

The Puppy's lips found Leo's half-hard cock and wolfed the lengthening bone down its throat.

In a pulse-pounding beat, Leo was rock-hard in the Puppy's slobbering warm mouth—filling it, it seemed, so completely that Leo could feel the ridges and ripples in the Puppy's throat.

True to its nature, the Puppy was a most playful cocksucker. The pup's weren't the careful orchestrations of the high-art cocksucker, or the vacuum intensity of the high-powered cocksucker. No, the Puppy sucked cock like it had been brought to it on a silver platter—its ideal biscuit. It licked and sucked and nuzzled and gnawed and growled at Leo's cock like it was a prize beyond all prizes, almost religious in its heat and importance.

Despite his slight shock, Leo quickly got into it, relishing the

Puppy's cocksucking romp. It wasn't long before Leo bucked his hairy, beary hips at the Puppy's suctioning mouth, growling and moaning like it was his first (or best) time.

Sitting in front of him, gold legs folded neatly under, the Puppy sucked and licked at Leo—all the while frictioning its own cock between its pressed-together legs. Its whining moans mixed with Leo's noises.

Champagne time!

With a primordial grunt and a backwater yelp, Leo came, splashing the back of the Puppy's throat with sweet (OK, salty and slightly bitter) come.

The Puppy thought, *Well, I had to thank you for letting me in, didn't I?* The puppy wiped its face with its paws, then licked the faint residue of come off them—for an instant more cat than dog.

After pulling himself from a near faint, Leo readjusted himself and glanced at the living room clock. *Jesus fuck,* he thought, *I'm late!*

The Puppy didn't want him to leave, that was for sure. But Leo got his way—as dog and Puppy owners always do—in the end.

Still, it wasn't easy going out, with the Puppy scratching mournfully at the front door to follow wherever Leo was going, then howling for his return.

Puppies, as anyone can tell you, love to get into trouble.

At least, Leo thought as he surveyed the house, *it didn't touch my Billie Holiday records.* Everything else, though.... Newspapers were tossed everywhere, as were his books. His CDs too were scattered all over. His bedclothes were completely off his bed and had been wadded into a new and probably much more comfortable, doggie bed on the floor. The hall was full of toilet paper. The kitchen was covered with coffee beans.

The Puppy thought, *Oops, think I might have overdid it.*

After several hours of straightening, Leo's place looked close, but not quite—he'd have to spend a few hours resorting his CDs—like it had before he'd left. He'd calmed down quite a bit, so when he faced the Puppy he was calm, controlled.

He also had a rolled-up newspaper.

"Bad dog!" he said, remembering to accentuate each syllable precisely, transmitting to the frisky beast the firmness of his words. He hauled it, whimpering and yapping into the bedroom (more elbow room).

"Bad dog!" he said again. Next to Leo, the poor little dog seemed small and innocent, its angelic face lit this time with fear and remorse and drawn by concern and pleading eyes.

Gotta be firm, Leo thought. Taking a good grip on the beast, he sat on the remade bed and forced the Puppy over his knees. "Bad dog!"

With the first swat the Puppy yelped so high and so sharp that Leo thought his ears would break. With the second, its yelp changed in tone, if not volume. The third elicited a bass rumbling growl—more pleasure than threat.

Four, five, six, seven, eight, nine. With each swat the Puppy barked and squirmed more and more in Leo's lap. For a while he thought the Pup would squirm its way free or fall off. But with a hook of his big arm, he dragged the Puppy to his chest.

The Puppy thought: *Oh, God, yes! Keep it up, big boy!*

Quickly, Leo lost count, relishing in the frisky pleasure the Puppy was getting out of its beating. Soon his arm was a blur and the impact and Puppy's squirming were one solid action. Something pressed into Leo's crotch. It took him a few seconds to realize it was the Puppy's cock, hard as iron, stroking up and down between Leo's thighs with each impact.

The beating reached a quick tattoo, Leo's arm a blur and the Puppy's wild squirms and thrashes one vibrant action. Leo broke into a sweat, and the Puppy's whole body quivered and quaked.

The Puppy thought, *Oh, yeah!*

Then the Puppy howled! Tilting its head back, it let loose a magnificent coyote howl of pure animal pleasure and pain. Then it collapsed, deflating into a simple little Puppy, a tired little beast.

Leo panted, heaving in his tight work overalls, seeing stars from his newspaper workout. His thighs, he suddenly realized, were wet with Puppy come. *Jesus, I think my arm's gonna fall off,* Leo thought to himself.

The Puppy thought, *Tomorrow I've gotta "have an accident." That was fucking great!*

Carefully, Leo lifted the Puppy and put it to bed in its little nest on the floor. Then, exhausted, he climbed into his own bed and fell asleep the instant his eyes closed.

In the morning, something warm and wet woke Leo.

He'd been happily flying (one of his favorite dreams), dimly aware of his house and the slight snoring of the Puppy when he became more and more aware of his cock and how incredibly hard it was.

Sleeping on his back as he usually did, he also became dimly aware of hot panting breath on his stomach, of the bedclothes dragged back.

The dream changed. Flying still, but flying through rain clouds that surrounded him with wet comfort—warm, wet comfort, especially around his cock.

Then it was *just* his cock. A wonderful sensation, ideal—the pressure, the heat, even the little puffs of hot breath on his stomach. Wonderful, heavenly, divine.... The good got better, then great.

Slowly the dream passed away, and almost as slowly, Leo awoke—to find the Puppy greedily sucking his cock.

Mouth wide, the Puppy opened his hot, tight throat and swallowed Leo down and down—surrounding him with pressure, heat, and passion.

It should be noted that Leo was not one who came all that easily in the morning, but that particular morning, with the Puppy working his cock like it was the only cock in the world, the most prized cock in the world, Leo moaned and grunted like a wild animal.

The Puppy was a Puppy possessed by a ravenous (rabid?) hunger for Leo's cock. It sucked, it licked, it swallowed, it nibbled, it rubbed, it stroked, it teased, it blew, it tickled, it kissed, and it jerked until Leo simply exploded in a glorious, world-shattering, body-quaking, shot.

After he had, the Puppy eagerly lapped up Leo's come and whined once (very happily) and yapped twice (very, very happily).

With the sparkles and panting still dancing in his eyes and his body, Leo rubbed the top of the Puppy's head and decided, then and there that this was a good dog and that, yes, he could he a good master to it. Leo said, "Goooooood boy!"

The Puppy thought, *Goooooood Master!*

What Ever Happened to...?

Betty used to be someone.

If she had an audience—pretty rare these days—she'd say, "I used to be Bouncin' Betty," and then she'd wait for remembrance to sweep across their faces (or, more likely, face). If none came, she would prompt, "*The* Bouncin' Betty, Dame of the Chateau, Queen of Halloween. Had my own disc: *Betty Got Back*. They played it looped at Folsom and Gay Day." Then she'd pull out her scrapbook. "This is a picture of me with Pussy; we played together the whole day. She said I was the best she'd ever seen. This is me at the Empress Ball. Here I am at Wigstock. I took first prize two years running; my trophy's over there on the mantel." On and on.

"Used to love to hit the ladies' johns around the city, especially on Folsom, Halloween, or Pride. Loved it! The *Weekly* even did a spot on me. Hang on, it's around here somewhere.... Ha! Here it is: 'King of the Queens.' Don't care for the title much, but I like the article. It even talks about the time I flashed the Republican Women's Auxiliary. Remember that? Well, darlin', they had this big hullabaloo about bullshit 'Family Values' so I got all Betty'd up and walked right into their meeting asking if I could use their damned ladies' room. Well, they got all offended and said it was 'for ladies only,' so I lifted my skirt and showed them my Special Surprise. I'd shaved my...well, you know, *organ*, and then had an arteest friend paint on a pussy: slit, clit, and all. So I tucked and flashed them. You should've seen their faces. Hit the fucking floor—excuse the unladylike word. But they did! They were so flabbergasted they even let me use their ladies' room. Took a mean ol' nasty dump in there too. Stunk up the place something awful." On and on.

Most people were polite. But eventually their eyes would glaze over and they'd start to sneak covert, then not so covert, glances at their watches. Others heeded the rumors and avoided her parlor altogether.

Sitting in her Victorian front room, Betty smoothed her white panty hose, straightened her little-girl pink pinafore, rubbed a smudge off her (now) spotless white patent leathers, fluffed her ruffles, and ran hesitant, slightly shaking fingers through her cascades of golden wig curls. Catching sight of the wrinkled face hiding beneath her rouged and painted face in her antique dressing mirror, she thought with a sigh, *The only thing worse than an ex-drag queen is an* old *ex-drag queen.*

"Here comes Mommy!"

Dressed especially for Betty (perfect glossy stilettos, antique-style white garters and hose, straight white A-line skirt, cat's-eye glasses and a high, but not too high, beehive wig), Joan came in, catching Betty leafing through her scrapbook and lingering, misty-eyed, over wrinkled flyers and faded clippings—as if her constant rereading of them had worn away the ink. Tapping Betty on the shoulder, she said, "Time to put those things away, dear," with venom laced into the sugar words.

When Betty didn't close her fragile scrapbook quickly enough, Joan reached down, yanked up Betty's pink pinafore, and attached two nasty plastic clothespins to her tiny nipples.

Hissing against the sudden pain, Betty did as she was told, moving carefully against the tugging ache from her nipples and pushing against the cloth back of her wheelchair. Involuntarily, her legs kicked out and knocked—but not over—the table. Realizing what she'd done, she snapped her eyes open and quickly scanned to make sure the breakfast things hadn't spilled onto her precious scrapbook. Luckily, the only spill was the coffee, and it had just made a muddy pool on its saucer.

"Next time," Joan said, kneeling and bouncing the clothespins up and down, "maybe you'll pay attention when I'm talking to you."

"Yes, Mommy."

Joan had never gotten to be someone.

Oh, sure, she had a great figure, perfectly made for pumps, sequins, feathers, and the proper but not extreme use of a girdle. But Joan had...other talents. Ones that didn't jibe with the femme mystique she could wear so well. At first, when she and Betty were an infant "item" in the drag scene, her talents were the cause of snickers and gossip: Betty tagging along on the arm of the big girl with the scary reputation and inclinations. They didn't snigger long, though. Not when talk of Joan's talents went from giggly rumors to awed worship. For a brief while (though Betty would never admit it) Joan's infamy had eclipsed Betty's glamorous fame. Joan had been speeding down the highway toward the Big Time and maybe a shot at crossover. "RuPaul with a whip" is what some called her.

She'd been—*was*—that good.

Speeding down the highway: Too accurate, that. Speeding, taillights out of nowhere, a faint alcohol daze, spinning, flying glass, spasming metal, the smell of gas and blood, the howl of sirens. And the deep, painful moans of Betty.

Betty lived: a life in her chair.

With the caring boredom of someone who's done it too many times, Joan snapped on a glove. After parting Betty's thighs with a flashing sweep she materialized a straight-razor with a mother-of-pearl handle and slashed away Betty's panty hose, exposing her fat cock and dark-furred balls.

Running her hand up and around Betty's ass and crotch, Joan checked her for rashes, all the while squeezing the twin clothespins on the old diva's nipples. "Has Mommy's Little Girl been good?" she said, acid playing through her words, lacing them with frustrated menace—a perfect acting job.

"I guess so, Mommy," Betty said in vulnerable tones, hanging her head in shame. Her voice was real.

"What do you mean, 'I guess so?'" Betty said, with theatrical anger, flipping at the clothespins and smiling with real satisfaction as Betty hissed in a breath against the jerking pain. "Don't you know if you've been good or not?"

"I-I played with myself." Betty said, head down lower if possible—chin to breastbone—a pink flush dying her cheeks a candy color.

"And what does that make you?"

"N-Naughty."

"And what happens to naughty little girls?"

Joan squirmed: humiliation, the pain from the clothespins, the acidic scorn.... "They get punished." Her voice was small and tight, squeezed out from where she was slouching, hiding.

"That's right. *Punished.* Do you like to get punished, Betty?"

Betty's squirms got more animated, more convulsive. Despite

the pins on her aching nipples, she reached up and tried to pull her pink pinafore down. "No," she said, shivering as the action put more strain on the clothespins.

"No one does, Betty. No one does. But you've been bad, haven't you? You've been a naughty little girl. You played with yourself against my orders!" Joan's shrill scream smashed around the dusty, claustrophobic room.

Shocked, Betty let go of her dress and the tension from the clothespins snapped it back up, showing her thickening cock. Humiliated, Betty blushed multiple shades of red and wrestled the dress down again, hissing like a tiny snake as the pins, again, bent back on her nipples. "I'm...(sniffle, sniffle)...sorry."

"Not good enough," Joan said, getting up and walking out the door. She returned a few minutes later carrying a large, domed silver serving tray. Seeing it, Betty whimpered pathetically.

"In this house," Joan said, sitting next to Betty's wheelchair, "we have rules. They may be harsh, they may be unfair, but they're the rules nonetheless. *My* rules. You agree?"

Scared eyes the size of hard-boiled eggs, Betty squeaked, "N-No."

"*You don't agree with me?*" Joan roared, a drag queen express train bearing down on little Betty tied to the tracks. "Of all the impudent, disrespectful—"

"No," Betty managed to fight out of herself, "I-I mean I don't want to—"

"But this is punishment, Betty. No one wants to be punished. But you played with yourself. You know the punishment for that."

A fatalistic veil fell over Betty. She took in a rasping breath, held it for a minute, and let it out in a oscillating whistle. She steeled herself, gathered herself, readied herself for an invisible crowd, audience, performance. "I know the punishment," she said.

"Then why do you keep doing it?" Joan asked, taking the dome off the tray.

"No," squeaked little frilly Betty.

"Oh, yes," Joan said, eyes lit with dancing maniac fires. "Very definitely yes."

Betty tried (sort of) to struggle as Joan pulled her dress up again. She stopped completely, though, and bent back in a stiff curve against the pain when Joan slapped the clothespins. As Betty made a harmonica sound through clenched teeth, Joan got out a soft wooden paddle and carefully, precisely, placed it under Betty's cock and balls—wedging it under Betty's thighs.

Betty started to whimper, but Joan ignored her as she dabbled her balls first with alcohol and then Betadine.

Next were two Velcro restraints. One went neatly around each of Betty's thin arms, holding her securely to her chair.

"Maybe next time you won't be so tempted..."

Betty nodded *yes* very hard, all but smacking her breastbone with her chin: an extremely enthusiastic *yes*!

Joan could have been a star. She could've been a *real* star. Anyone who'd ever seen her thought the same thing: she was so talented, so precise, that she could've gone pro, become a legend. She had a feel for it, and—God—to see her face as she got out her needles, you knew she had a *taste* for it. She loved it.

Carefully, she put on her gloves. Moving like a geisha, she uncapped a 20-gauge and got down to where she could really see Betty's cock and balls. "Breathe," she whispered, pushing Betty's thighs apart as far as she could, stretching her scrotum until the dark red skin turned a pale pink.

Betty breathed in twice, three times. Then Joan put the needle through.

Coughing out a deep primordial tone that belonged more to a sweat lodge than a Grand Dame of the Empress Ball, Betty squished her eyes shut.

"Very nice, baby," Joan said, picking up another needle. "Very, very nice, my sweet little girl."

"Thank you, Mommy," Betty panted, preparing herself for the next.

Joan slid in the next needle: just the right amount of pressure to pierce Betty's scrotum and slide it into the wooden paddle. Joan's fingers, as always, *danced*. She had a way with sharps: They were her instrument of choice. Hands flashing like a magician, she made the amphlets appear, then, popping off their clear plastic caps, *disappear* into Betty's scrotum.

Joan could have been a star: She was *that* damned good.

For Betty, it really was magic. Black, white, gray...*magic*. The way Joan made the needles appear—materializing out of nowhere—and then vanish with a rolling wave of pain, like the thunderclap following a flash of lightning: pure magic. One needle quick, one needle slow, one needle quick, one needle quick— varying the delivery, the details, to keep Betty from falling back into an expected routine. She was on pins and needles, literally, waiting for when/where/how the next needle tip would come— right side, right side, left side, right side. Her expectations and fear made the pain that much sharper, that much more brittle and jagged. Betty tasted it like blood (and had to run a quick tongue around the inside of her mouth to see if she'd bitten herself; she hadn't): a sharp, metallic kind of broken expectation. It went from fear and dipped almost into terror. She didn't know where the next needle was going to land, what the next kind of pain would be.

All the time, Joan was talking: "You're a slutty girl, aren't you? You can't hide it from Mommy, you know. Mommies can tell. I can tell. Your panties are wet, aren't they? Dripping wet. And this, your clit, is nice and big and hard, isn't it? Wet panties. Hard clit. You're a slut. You're thinking of getting fucked, right now. You're sitting there while I punish you for rubbing your pus and you're thinking of getting fucked. That's now much of a slut you are. I'm sitting her jamming fucking needles into your cunt and you're thinking of getting fucked. That's a slut, girl. That's a righteous slut, to take pins in your pus and still want to fuck. Look at this clit! That's the biggest clit I've ever seen, and Mommy's seen some fat fucking clits in her day, girl! This is a fucking huge clit..." WHACK! Joan backhanded Betty's cock hard enough to hurt, but not hard enough to tear the amphlets. A true artist. "This is a monster, slutty clit. You're dripping, aren't you, girl? Yeah, I can tell. I can tell that you're just aching to get fucked, all wet and open and ready. Yeah. I can tell..."

Eight needles. Betty's cock wasn't going anyplace, even though it was trying. Painfully hard, it strained and pulled against the pinning needles. But Joan's placement was so perfect it could just reach its height before feeling the painful tugs of the amphlets. No tearing, not a lot of blood, just a ring of deep ache around Betty's cock and balls. Joan definitely had true talent. Star, *legend* potential.

"Bet you taste good, girl. Bet you taste real good. Bet you'd like your Mommy more than anything to taste your sweet pus. Bet you ache for it, more than the fucking pins. Yeah, I know you do. I can smell it on you like cheap fucking perfume. Toilet water. You must have really laid on the *Come Suck Me* stuff this morning, slut, 'cause it sure as shit stinks on you something awful. You reek of it, bitch. My fucking head is just full of the smell of you wanting my mouth on your clit. But if you want it so bad, you have to ask for it."

"Please..."

"Beg for it."

"Pretty please..."

"Whimper. Come on, you've done it before. Do it again."

"With sugar on it..."

"Such a fucking slut," Joan said, reaching around and behind her to the pile of supplies on the silver tray. In a flash—more magic—she had something in her mouth. In another flash—still more magic—she had her mouth over Betty's cock. She was very, very good with more than "sleight of hand," because Betty never saw, or felt, the Gold Circle slide over her throbbing dick. All she felt was her Bitch Mommy, Joan, drop her wide open mouth onto her straining and screaming-with-pain cock.

Joan's mouth was a hot wet blanket. The best kind of mouth. True talent. Good in a dress? A guy in hose. Good voice? Gravel pouring out of a dump truck. Good dancer? Sore toes from the Ball to the bus stop. Joan's skill was in her needles, her canes, crops, whips, clamps, ropes, and her mouth. Especially her cock-sucking mouth.

She could have been a star. Well, she was—for Betty.

Two of the needles pulled free—they vanished before they could poke anything—and the six others strained and all but tore Betty's screaming scrotum as she came, jetting so hard and hot and heavy that her come felt like hot lead squirting into Joan's mouth.

Betty heaved and panted for what must have been a minute, but felt like hours, until her dick lost its erect weight in Joan's mouth. With her audience done, Joan put away her pigeons (she took the clothespins off with a deep, rumbling moan from Betty); she tucked away her top hat (she quickly pulled the needles, swabbed the points with alcohol and Betadine); and she put away the rest of her magic tricks as well (she removed the restraints and gave Betty a quick sponge with a warm rag and a sweet kiss on her dewed forehead).

Getting up to make them both a snack, Joan felt Betty's thin hand catch the hem of her only slightly ruffled dress.

"Don't go yet," Betty said in a tired but happy voice.

Joan smiled, a crease on her face, and crouched next to Betty's chair. "What," she said with a small laugh, "and give up show business?"

Coyote and the Less-Than-Perfect Cougar

They said, with whispering conspiracy as well as deep, booming certainty, that Wily could, would, and did sell anything to anyone: sunlight on a cloudless, hot day; water during a thunderstorm; ice at the North Pole.

They who said this were various residents of Albuquerque, New Mexico, United States of America. They didn't say it lot—there were, after all, other things to talk about in Albuquerque. There was, for instance, the common "Damn it's hot," the not-quite-as-common-but-still-quite-common "Have you ever felt it this hot?" and the rare-but-still-common-enough "It's hot enough to melt pennies."

John had been in town for three months, seven days, some hours, and—no doubt—quite a turn of minutes. Therefore, he had heard, any number of times, "Damn, it's hot"; "Have you ever felt it this hot?"; and "It's hot enough to melt pennies." But he'd not heard one solitary word about Wily of the Rafael Dumont La Cruz Rehabilitated Motor Works; he hadn't heard of Wily's ability to wheel and deal a man's nose off his face, his wife for a kidney bean, or air from his lungs. So when he drove his tomato-soup '79

151

Cougar toward the lot he actually thought to himself, *I'll bet I can talk myself into a sweet deal.*

John—as has been stated in this narrative—had only been in town a short while. One could say he still had the dust of Barstow, Calif., on his cheap boots, that the air of the refinery there still lingered in his curly brown locks, that the sight of wooden clapboard houses still lurked in the glimmering of his pale blue eyes. One could also say he was ripe for the plucking.

The Rafael Dumont La Cruz Rehabilitated Motor Works was located midway down Santa Ana Avenue. The lot was a narrow strip of mushy asphalt stretched along the avenue on one side. Beyond the lot, separated by a sad, sagging chain-link fence, were many acres (ownership unknown) of dead grass, yellow sand, and rocks. Population: one very large crow and many mice.

On the lot were two dozen vehicles of dubious quality, ranging from a classic Ford Mustang with an obvious bad bondo job on its right front fender to a Ford LTD with a crappy interior, to a Volkswagen in surprisingly excellent condition. There was also a beauty of Detroit mechanical skill: a Dodge Daytona—a machine of thunderous glory, a high-octane god of a two-lane Heaven. Such was its shattering, muscular glory that it seemed to move, to roar and speed, even while cold and idle.

Also on the lot was a sagging, aluminum-sided trailer—of which there are many in Albuquerque. In its fly-specked and dirty window was a sign proclaiming that the Lord Above was the only person to whom the establishment would extend credit. Next to that was a ramshackle garage composed of rusting corrugated iron and peeling, cheap paint—stuffed to capacity with the greasy carcasses of cars in even worse condition than those on the lot.

On a rather temperate day—for Albuquerque—John drove up in his slightly knocking, slightly listing, possibly leaking '79

Cougar. He parked it snugly against the curb. The sun was high, the sky clear, and the wind a soft breath, barely enough to lazily move the dirty plastic pennants that sagged across the lot.

John had spent a good part of the previous day washing, waxing, tinkering with, and, in general working to present his machine in the best possible light. He succeeded only marginally, as the improvements were obviously superficial.

A word, or several, about John: As stated, the dust of Barstow still clung to him, but unlike the tanned and leather people of that distant town, it had not worked its way into his soul, his essence. His skin, yes, was dry and thick, but hadn't achieved the leathered texture that seemed to insulate the people of Barstow, as well as those of Albuquerque. His was a pleasant, working skin. His face was common but not exceptional: a person's face, and not the superficial, illusionary beauty that many possess. His nose was thin, with a slight point. His hair was brown and curly and long in the back. He sported a simple mustache, a perfectly matching stroke of brown hair. His body was broad and strong—like his face, a person's body. He had an attractiveness that reached out through his common components and made you look at him and smile. He looked as he was, the honesty of him showing, obvious.

After parking his coughing, hesitant, musically pinging car, John got out, took a slow, deep breath to steady his slightly quaking nerves, shaded his eyes against a sudden burst of hostile glare from the hard sun far above, and tripped, neatly and perfectly, over a low chain looping up to rusting pipes and then down to the dusty street—all around the lot.

"Whoa there, friend," said a quick and playful voice, as someone strong caught John's arm, kept him from spilling onto the sidewalk. "Mustn't scuff one's knees on the hard and unforgiving ground."

"Much obliged," John said, in no way injured but startled nonetheless by the quickness of his near-spill.

"Just think of it as one of those little courtesies we toss in at the Rafael Dumont La Cruz Rehabilitated Motor Works. You know...air fresheners shaped like pine trees, calendars the size of a postage stamp, key chains with the company name worn off before you stick it in your pocket. That kind of thing."

Despite himself, John smiled at the man whose hand still clutched, pleasantly, his upper arm.

"Wily," the man said. "Commonly referred to hereabouts as a purveyor of used transportation. Pleased to make your acquaintance." Wily released John's arm and clasped—firm and dry—his hand in a vigorous, pumping shake.

John smiled, a deer caught in the headlights of Wily's words. "John. Nice to meet you."

A word, or several, about Wily: Wily's face was...well, there wasn't anything exactly evil about his nose, mouth, lips, chin, forehead, hair, or eyes. He didn't appear vindictive or cruel—it was more that he looked slippery or sly. You couldn't look exactly straight at Wily because Wily was somehow too slick to be seen dead-on. You had to approach him from some other angle, absorb him from spare details because the whole of him was just too smooth to see at once. But what details Wily had were pleasant. His skin was a native tan, marking him as one of the many tribal mutts to be seen around those parts those days. His hair was coal and midnight—seen only by reflections. His face was a playful dance of twinkling elements, a slightly bulbous nose, full lips, too-straight and too-clean teeth—a brilliant yellow sparkle from a single gold incisor. And his eyes: Much could be said about his eyes. The rest of him danced away from clear examination, but his eyes were clear and clean—too much so, as if they saw way too much. If he looked at you with them...as he was looking at

John...it was like he was drinking you, gulping down the essence of you. He had a dishonest aspect, but his eyes saw truth, every kind of truth, from every kind of angle.

"Well, now, sir, might I inquire as to what would bring an obviously cultured gentleman such as yourself down to these less-than-civil parts on this most magnificent morning?" Wily said, playfully extracting himself from the handshake with a wicked smile that displayed his gold tooth like a burst of sunlight.

"I came down to see, um, what you might give me for, you know..." John nodded, suddenly disarmed and shy at his Cougar and its rippling seams, sunlight flickers of pits in the windshield, bleaching paint, and crust of rust wrapping around the wheel wells.

Wily laughed, a grumbling animal sound that made John take a step back. You might have expected something witty and urbane, something slippery and clever, but this sound was feral and unfettered. It was surprising. "Well, then, we'll just have to see what it is you've brought to our fine and dignified establishment. In the meantime, feel free to browse our fine selection of automobile excellence. Allow your mind to slide behind the wheel of our beautifully engineered dreams, to travel the roads you've always yearned to travel. I assure you, you'll not leave here today in this machine that brought you."

With that, Wily rolled back his sleeves, showed John that he had nothing up them, and slowly, rather methodically examined John's car.

John watched, studying the play of Wily's muscles under the cheap-appearing blue suit, the way his thighs worked as he moved, the way his shoulders twisted, the manner of his sweeping, theatrical movements. John saw him as a dancer, a preacher, a painter, a magician about to make something appear—or, he thought after Wily spoke, *disappear*.

Wily turned away from the car and faced John. There was something about his face, something drawn and deep. Something no longer light and dancing. John felt sadness drop through him, weigh him down with stones and drown him somewhere dark and deep: "Alas, John," said Wily. "What we have here, in the parlance of the rehabilitated vehicle trade, is a 'less-than-perfect Cougar.' A Cougar, it is my sincere displeasure to state, that the ages, the road, and the universe itself have ground down, stripped of everything except the barest trace of automotive life."

The sadness was indeed a weight, a stone, in John's gut. The world lost a bit of its gleam. John's dreams of driving something mighty and powerful off the lot evaporated with Wily's words, with the firm and slightly sad expression on Wily's face.

But then—a magician pulling something out his hat, a preacher curing what ails you, a painter making something from nothing, a dancer leading you through complex steps—Wily smiled.

Wily said, gold tooth glimmering like light from a billion angels' wings, "Don't despair, John. Don't let reality weigh you down, for—and I'm sure you'll echo this sentiment once you hear it—the world is not cold, hard logic, facts, figures, and amounts. The world, you see, is people. And people can do miracles with the harshness of the world.

"In fact," he continued, putting a more-than-fatherly, more-than-brotherly arm around John's broad shoulders and giving him a more-than-brotherly, more-than-fatherly squeeze, "we might be able to come to an agreement as to where you might leave this fine establishment of rehabilitated automobiles with something very close to the dream you no doubt had when you arrived."

John didn't say anything. He didn't need to: His excited eyes spoke for him.

"What I'm proposing to you is, shall we say, a trade…"

"He's not human, you know. He might look it, but it's a trick. He's good at that. Tricking. Very good. He's had eternity to practice," Crow said.

The first stone missed, tossed up a small puff of yellowish dust far into the dry, dead field behind the Rafael Dumont La Cruz Rehabilitated Motor Works.

Crow, all disarrayed feathers and blazing red eyes, danced across the top of the solitary telephone pole—bare of even broken insulators, let alone wires. "I don't know what he's promised, but he won't deliver. OK, he might, but he'll still screw you. Wait and see."

The second stone hit the pole, a deep wooden *thunk* that rang surprisingly loud across the empty space. Too low, though. It didn't even interrupt Crow's dance, or his chatter.

"Why do you think I'm here?" asked Crow. "He fucked me over. He'll fuck you over. I'm just waiting for a good shot at him, that's all. And now he's got you out here doing his dirty work. I tell you, don't trust him!"

The third stone went spiraling out of control, clanging against an iron spike.

"Don't you know who he is? Can't you figure it out? Think about it. His name is *Wily*, for Gitche Manitou's sake. You're going to be hurt. Or tricked real *nasty*."

The next was close, also ranging the wooden bell of the old telephone pole, this time with a higher tone, frequency, hitting closer to the top. Crow stopped and gave a very crowlike squawk, followed by a flap of great black wings.

"Fine, fine, FINE! Have it your own way—see if I care. Just

don't come crawling back to me: 'Oh, poor me. Oh, sorry me. Look what happened to me.' Ha! See what happens."

The next stone was dead-on—thunking into Crow's great, black body with an echoing, meaty impact. Again cawing sharp and loud, the bird extended its charcoal wings and beat down hard, flying off, leaving behind only a few ashen feathers, twisting as they fell to the dry ground.

"So what did he offer you, huh? An arrow that always meets its mark? A night with Bear Woman? Singing stones? The Bones of Big Monster? Must be somethin' mighty special for you to be chasing little old me with that damned broom," Mouse said.

It might have been because Mouse was so small and his words so honest, or it might have been that the day was getting long—the sky turning softly purple—and John was getting tired, or it might have been that John was simply starting to wonder. So he did, in fact, stop and really, quickly, think. What *had* Wily offered?

Wily's words fell quicksilver through his mind. Images played, chrome and high octane, shown with sly words and the wave of a tanned hand—treasures that could, for a favor, a trade, perhaps be his: a classic Ford Mustang with an obvious bad bondo job on its right front fender, a Ford LTD with a crappy interior, a Volkswagen in surprisingly excellent condition. And the Dodge Daytona.

But how to explain this to a talking mouse? Finally, opting for simplicity, he said, "A new car."

"Oh, that explains it. I perfectly understand now why you're trying to kill me with a broom. For a car. Oh, yes, perfectly understandable. That completely makes sense."

"But you see..." John started to explain.

"No need to explain," said Mouse, a tiny voice in the vast, dark, greasy garage of the Rafael Dumont La Cruz Rehabilitated Motor Works. "We've all been there—on the receiving end of that smiling critter, Coyote. He's a slick one. Not one to trust in the least. Guess it's just your turn is all."

Crouched on the hardness of the cement floor, John dug about with his broom.

"Not that he's completely bad. Let's just say he's...Coyote. He'll do ya, no doubt. But sometimes he kinda does you a favor too. Nothing that makes up for being fucked with, but not completely bad either."

"I know what you mean," said John, more to keep Mouse talking while he dug around with the broom than because he did know.

"Well, I'm glad you understand. Because before you know it, that's what's gonna happen to you. And after, who knows? Maybe you'll be staking out the son of a bitch, waiting to get a piece of him, dealing with some asshole trying to ream with you a goddamned broom! You're on your own, kid. Just don't say I didn't warn you!" said Mouse from down where the corrugated walls met the concrete floor. Dropping down and thrusting the broom, all John could see was a hole leading outside. And a scattering of Mouse turds.

"Crow?"

"Flapping off to parts unknown."

"Mouse?"

"Hightailing it away."

"Marvelous! Simply astounding, John! A perfectly incredible

performance!" Wily clapped a strong arm around John and pulled him into a sideways macho hug. "It fills my heart with joy that you've done so well. I set before you two difficult tasks and what do you bring me, John? Two glorious successes! Excellent, John, I do have to say."

John, surprisingly, blushed a red that nearly matched the bleeding, setting sun shining through the small trailer windows.

"I'm pleased, John, and do you know what I do when I'm pleased? Any idea? None at all? Well, I'll tell you, John, I'll tell you straight and true—I get a good case of generosity! That's right, John, a heaping bout of that wondrous malady—the glorious sickness of generosity."

Quickly, Wily took John and towed him to the grimy window overlooking the lot. "Look there, John. See those gorgeous examples of the art of the automobile? See that sampling of the American horseless carriage? Let your eyes glide along the classical lines of that cherry Mustang (pay no attention to the bondo), see the brutal magnificence of that Ford LTD (don't worry about the interior), and that delightful little charmer of a Volkswagen (that leaks oil—but not a lot of oil). Radiate in the pure elegance, the perfectly engineered ferocity of the height of Detroit muscle, that Dodge Daytona (it'll cost you a future in gas and speeding tickets). Look at them, John. Look at them all and know that any of them, any of these beauties could be yours—yes, yours—as the result of the dizzying attack of generosity you have brought upon my usually stingy self."

John was...awed. Staring out the streaked window, his eyes darted back and forth and back and forth while his heart hammered in his chest. Options and possibility clouded his mind with a white noise of potential—a beautiful storm of choices. This one? That one? This one? That one? There was no way he'd ever be able to decide. Each choice, each car, was glory.

"Or," Wily said, in a simple, low voice, "you can have something..." he paused, a massive weight of a moment, "...*really* special.

"Now when I use those words, those simple little words, *really special*, I don't mean your simple really special. I mean a really special that pushes the highest potential of those words, that touches the ceiling of their concepts. What I mean is truly, honestly, *really special*."

John was entranced, captured by the phantasmagoria of Wily's words. In a flash of imagination, gone were the tired little dreams of the paltry machines decaying just beyond the cheap tin walls of the office. Instead, formless yet thrilling fantasies rolled through his consciousness—ghostly giants of pleasure that he, having not yet experienced them, could only guess at. So it was natural that, after hearing Wily speak as he had, John said, "Go on."

"I can barely put into words," Wily said, eyes sparkling like firelight on gems, gold tooth glimmering, "the glory of what I am offering. In fact, even if I had the words I would not speak them, because doing so would anchor the magnificence of my offer, dragging it to the earth."

John swallowed, hard. "I'm interested," he said.

"And so you should be. For what I'm offering is nothing less than, dare I say it, *incredible*." Wily continued after a sufficient pause, "May I presume, John, that you might be willing to, say, perform one more simple—oh, so simple—task to receive this truly, absolutely, positively, incredible thing?"

John thought—as much as he could think, with his mind profoundly mumbled by racing images of indescribable delight—and said, "Yeah," in a sleepy, shocked voice.

To which Wily said, smiling broad and porcelain, "Then...take off your pants."

John had never traveled that road. Sure, he was a man who'd seen the world, at least the bits from Barstow to Albuquerque, so he knew that way was there. But it was one thing to drive by and see that road, stretching off toward god-knew-what, and quite another to actually turn and follow that route.

Still, to be fair, it would have been wrong to say John hadn't looked down that road a few times, with a certain amount of curiosity and excitement and wonder about where it might lead, where it might take him.

It would also have been wrong—completely, utterly wrong—to say that if he had taken that road he would have seen the sight that he saw that day in the office/trailer of the Rafael Dumont La Cruz Rehabilitated Motor Works.

"My God," John said, and thought, as Wily dropped his pants.

"You are too kind," Wily responded, smiling, flashing his gold tooth, as he reached out to put a smooth hand around John's hard cock. "Besides, John, I might say the same."

John blushed, not for the action—an electric spark as Wily's tanned hand wrapped with sensual delicacy around his pulsing shaft—but for the compliment: John was blessed, he knew, with a more-than-average sized cock. Not a monster—nothing that would make women (and now men?) scream and faint, but still a delightful surprise, a sexual prize in his pants.

John liked his cock, was quite pleased with both its length and its general shape and appearance. He had a slightly dim forest of hair, something that tickled those who liked to get down close. Cut—he didn't miss that fantasy piece of skin—with a fat head that, when he was really charged, as he was in that trailer, became a pleasantly purple bulb.

John's purple bulb that bobbed up and down under the firm yet soft strokes of Wily.

Then, before John was even sure of what was occurring, Wily dropped to his knees, taking John quickly down that road not yet traveled. Wily had a surprisingly—the good kind of surprise—warm mouth. Almost hot, almost steaming. So shocked was John by the quickness of the sensation and the temperature that he almost cried out, almost let sounds bubble up his throat and escape his lips. *Almost*—because he really didn't. Instead the sound expired somewhere between his guts and his lips and changed into a simple, slight moan.

There was no argument (definitely not from John) that Wily knew exactly what he was doing: With a practiced and passionate ballet of tongue, lips, roof of mouth, and, yes, even the frightening hardness of his teeth, including a brief, chilled contact of the gold one, he relished John's cock. And John—head back, back arched—moaned and bucked with little motions of his hips.

It was to Wily's credit that John went...somewhere else. He was dimly aware that Wily was working his cock, sucking, licking, kissing and playfully biting, but it was a distant knowledge, a delightful memory. John was actually floating somewhere over the tiny, dim trailer, watching the sunset as the rushes and surges of pleasure vibrated through his immaterial body.

Near orgasms rose through him, like breaths from some great mouth—as if John were being inflated (higher toward that bleeding, setting sun) and deflated (sinking back toward his body). He was being brought up, drawn down through the beautifully orchestrated movements of Wily's mouth on his cock. Falling, rising, he became aware as he flew on crests of almost-orgasms that his come too was rising and falling, nearing the point of explosion and then being drawn back into his humming, aching body by the perfect skill of Wily.

Then, when John thought that his body would open, bloom with an unstoppable scream of frustrated ecstasy, Wily lifted him higher and higher and higher with the power of his lips, his tongue, the corrugated sensation of the roof of his mouth, and the hard ridge of his teeth. And, finally, with a shout that rattled the cheap tin walls of the trailer, John, late of Barstow, Calif., came.

And boy, did he. It would be a lie to say he came gallons, but not a big one. Cream, man cream, spurted and pulsed from the head of John's cock and into the lapping mouth of an equally moaning Wily. Licking as if John's jism were the tastiest of delicacies, Wily cleaned him thoroughly, not stopping until John's cock was as clean as the day he was born. And still as hard as he'd ever been.

John, floating somewhere high and good, heard Wily say something. Part of him, a part that still was aware of the world of his fleshy body, understood and responded to the request. John, safe to say, was far along that road. He grunted and moaned as Wily entered him. A little fear reached through his excitement and said, *Remember how big he is?*

Big? Damned yes: an earthen, crimson pole jutting out from an improbable thicket of coarse hair. An uncut head the size of a pale onion—enough to bring tears to anyone's eyes. A bobbing monster of a cock that would have been frightening any other time.

So John thought to that little fearful voice, *Shut up and enjoy the ride.*

To Wily's credit, he was careful and cautious. To John's credit, he tried to keep from throwing himself back onto Wily's terrifying member. Finally, between their mutual cautions, they moved into a delicious, humming, moaning rhythm.

In seconds they weren't John, from Barstow, and Wily,

Coyote, but rather a moving ballet of flesh, skin, and delight. In and out—sliding, moving, pulsing, pumping to oscillating moans, grunts, and sighs.

Together, they went where John had been, alone, just a moment before—balls of golden delight floating high above the reality of the trailer, the dusty street, the setting sun, and the planet earth.

Like all incredible, mind-blowing, earth-shattering, beautiful, awe-inspiring things...it had to end. But like few incredible, mind-blowing, earth-shattering, beautiful, awe-inspiring things, it ended with something that was beyond (you guessed it) incredible, mind-blowing, earth-shattering, beautiful, or awe-inspiring.

Imagine all of your best comes pasted into one single fuck. That would be close to Wily and John's experience. But only close.

John had never, ever, felt anything like it.

Wily, who was Coyote, had, of course. But only because he was the one who'd stolen Big Monster's heart, made love to Spider Woman, taught Sparrow to sing, and stolen the sun.

Then it was over—in the past. John lay sprawled on the dusty floor of the trailer, a pile of tired muscles and a slightly aching asshole. Slowly, he became aware that he was there, still in that trailer, on that floor. But the ringing of the orgasm was still too wonderfully loud for him to care.

Finally, after the sun had slipped into night, he got up, confused, alone, and rather sore. Adjusting himself, he stumbled into the vacancy of the Rafael Dumont La Cruz Rehabilitated Motor Works. Gone was the Ford Mustang with the bad bondo job, the Ford LTD with the crappy interior, and the Volkswagen in surprisingly excellent condition. Gone too was beautiful Dodge

Daytona. Nothing there but an empty lot with dirty pennants flapping in a turgid breeze.

Even his less-than-perfect Cougar was gone—only a fresh slick of oil marked where it had been.

Of Wily, of Coyote—because John was now absolutely certain that was who he'd always been—there was no sign.

No, wait, a tanned piece of skin, a fragment of leather, tumbling by in that turgid breeze. Shocked, stunned, John bent and picked it up.

In charcoal—as if scrawled before a fire that had been burning since Coyote stole Big Monster's heart, made love to Spider Woman, taught Sparrow to sing, and stole the sun—it said: *I hope you enjoyed my truly, absolutely, positively, incredible thing, John. It wasn't exactly a fair trade for your less-than-perfect Cougar—but we'll call it even.*

John kept that piece of skin, that note, for a day or so. But then one day when he went looking for it he was gone. The memories, though, lasted much, much longer.

Counting

Overheated from the humid kitchen, the front windows fogged with condensation then streaked with clarity where drops raced down. The café wasn't exactly a place to show restraint, to bottle a smile, a smirk, a loud laugh. The place was safe, after all; the Militia were cracking heads in the Tenderloin, but this was the Castro/Mission—a world away. Still, Tubal was calm when I told him. No excitement. No pleasure. Not angry that *I* was telling *him* about it.

This was our space, not theirs.

"Cut his balls off, stuck 'em in his mouth," I said, "and sewed it shut. Don't know if he was still kicking when they did it, but he probably was. Hell, why go through the work if he was dead?"

Even the papers called it "an atrocity," a "brutal and senseless act of cruelty" in halting, official English. Hundreds dead in a food riot, "necessary means," secret raids, friends missing, "keeping the public order."

One civil servant accused of child rape—in whispers at bus stops, on illegal networks, in the endless lines for bread or clean water. Found with cock and balls stuffed in his mouth, stitched up.

"Number seven," I said. "In his blood on the wall."

The only thing Tubal said was, "I wonder how high it'll go."

I was lucky. I was safe because I was a necessity. My covert peccadilloes were overlooked because I was a system hack, the guy who kept the local Citicore network from delivering Sanskrit instead of the analyzed and digitized results of the Tokyo exchange.

I had acquired my skill because my father had managed to keep me in a Militia school until I was old enough to read, and because when he was gone, my street friends had opened some doors and shown me where the old info was kept.

Masoqui, the taciturn and finely sculpted Serb who ran the local Citicore office, knew I was gay—worse than dirt. He could've, should've turned me in. After all, he was a devout New Muslim. Rules were rules, God was in His Heaven, and the police squeal line was a speed dial on his personal phone.

Unless, of course, you knew how to keep the machines working.

So I stayed in the dark, with bundles of stiff fiber-optic cable and humming junction boxes smelling faintly of ozone and cooking plastic. I worked my magic, stayed hidden in the walls, and survived.

I had been going through one of the old, burned-out wrecks in the Mission. The info I'd scammed had said it used to be an auxiliary trunk line for the old telephone company, before the

Militia had rolled down Folsom and blown it as a makeshift fire-break—a little stronghold against the scattered pot-shots of the old Muni police.

The building's upper stories were a gap-toothed shell, the lower floors buried under complex bergs of broken concrete and twisted steel. In the days before the Crazy, the navigable floors would've housed dozens of families. Now it was empty.

I found a hall that was bare, cleaned of broken concrete and smelling of brackish water and, faintly—the ghost of gaunt children with bloated bellies—urine.

One end was blocked by a solid steel door. Scratches and dents showed where the desperate had tried to force their way inside. The desperate, though, had starved or been killed before they could succeed.

Even with the power arm I'd checked out of the tool library it took me two hours to pry the door open. Then another two to clear away the rubble from the main junction boxes. It was worth it, though. Like bales of glassy hair, bundles of fiber and fine wire packed the lower level. Enough to keep the San Francisco Citicore running for a long time.

I had just started with the company back then, drawn purely by the hatred and desperation in the eyes of the old Serb, Masoqui. "You fix, I pay you," was all he said after showing me the cracked casings of the interlink junctions and the stained, frayed, and bent fibers. I said I would. "In two day," he said. I'd agreed. The only alternative was another week in the Unemployed Shelter, then soon to the heavy fighting in the Northern Wilds— I had been two weeks from military conscription.

It was getting dark as I finally made my way out with my treasure of lost technology, the sunset powerful and dull orange against the saw-toothed skyline. I remembered people talking about when the city had been tall and gleaming. State-of-the-art, back when there was art. But all I'd ever known was the jumble of five-story buildings, rooftops jagged where the Militia had sheared them off. Not enough power for lifts, not enough food for the inhabitants—so make the city smaller. Or so the militia had decided.

I could just make out the Citicore building, one of a half-dozen buildings that still managed some precarious skyscraping. Wet feet in shoes two sizes too big, stomach beyond hungry and now slightly distended, bundles of fiber wrapped around my shoulders, my waist, I pushed and pulled myself out. My thoughts were alive with little dreams (the only kind anyone could really afford back then): clean food, maybe medicine, reasonable clothes, a room somewhere. Maybe even enough for wine rather than turpentine.

Guns: one of the first things the Militia had stripped from the city, then the state. Only the Militia produced them now, used them now—on criminals and deviants too slow to hide. The gun was a fear symbol: A stylized pistol on a square of red against a field of pure, unblemished white hung from the stones of City Hall.

The first time I saw it I thought it was an old pipe. Then the realization came. I sat down, lowered my eyes, and stitched my fingers together behind my head: baser reflexes, familiar voices at food riots when I was a boy, and now food riots when I'm much older, screaming *Sit or die.*

"What are you doing here?"

I tensed, expecting a bullet.

He repeated himself, crunching over to me on the broken stone. I shook, rustling the bundles of fibers.

"Scavenging? That's all you're doing. Shit." the expletive carried the sound of release, and I felt the barrel of the pistol, the hot dot of his aim, fall from my head. "You could get killed for that, you know."

"I know. It's for a job. Parts to fix a fiber optical telecom link." My words were crisp, stuttering, explaining way too much.

He hauled me along by grabbing one of the loops of line. "Come on, you can't hang around here."

I looked at him, Tubal, for the first time. My height, but stocky and well-formed. I could see his muscles even through his gray Maintenance jumpsuit. Bald. A salt-and-pepper mustache, bristly and stiff. His eyes, I found later, were so blue as to be closer to steel. His teeth, also later, weren't jagged tombstones on an eroding hillside for once. Only a single wayward incisor, leaning backward. His breath smelled of lemons, and I thought instantly of money and the exotic things it could buy.

Too frightened to do anything but follow, hauling the power arm and the cables that would help me fix Mr. Masoqui's fiber optical telecom link station, Tubal led me out of Old Town, up to Mission. At the Militia checkpoint he smiled and showed that nearly perfect smile to the young Militia men. Offering them slim black sticks of their intense tobacco, he made small talk with them—keeping me under his arm, protected. I was numb from the pistol, and heard ringing in my ears—the bullet that was never fired. It was a zombie he escorted through the battery-sellers, the water-filterers, the drug markets. A zombie spared from death.

Days later, in my dark corner of Mr. Masoqui's building, I realized I'd been hard as a rock the whole time.

The fibers did the job—enough at least to make the stone of Mr. Masoqui's face smile tightly with satisfied self-interest. My niche was won. Still, I didn't move from the alley at 16th and Guerrero, from the old blue Americom shipping crate, for nearly a month. All the cash Masoqui slipped me went into more fiber; ancient, corroded connectors; and water-stained and nearly illegible ancient manuals from before the Militia, the Reformed Western States, and New Muslim.

When I did move, my possessions in a canvas shopping bag, it was to a tiny room in an old Victorian: ancient plaster walls run with moisture, stained yellow, brown, and black from the candles and lanterns of previous tenants. My landlord was Chinese, an elusive figure who only descended from his iron-barred fortress on the third floor to extract the weekly rent. Everyone was in their rooms on Fridays, waiting for the soft knock of Mr. Sung. Failure to be present or not have the required 300 Sols would mean a visit from the Militia.

Of me, Sung had no concern or opinion, except that I was always there on Fridays with my money. I could've been collecting the genitals of children for all he cared. I was for him what I was for Masoqui: a resource. Everything else was immaterial.

My first month, I was caught outside in a riot. I hadn't been there long enough to recognize the neighborhood's telltales, the rhythm of the block: when the stores would be allowed to open, when the local Militia had to make its quota, when the insane would be released from their camps to clean and scour the streets of anything valuable or edible.

I was walking back from work, head lost in a maze of junctions, cross-connectors, light-boosts, and mirror-boxes, trying to deduce a ghost echo in the inner-office trunk lines. I was too full of Mr. Masoqui's system to notice the closed windows or the quiet. Then...running people. Seeing them sprint past, chests rising, breath fogging the cool evening, looking behind as they ran, I turned as well.

A wave rounded Market—a panicked sea of old Militia coats flapping, feet wrapped in threadbare carpets, eyes red and desperate. A thousand, probably more, screaming and crying as people do only when they've tasted panic. I got no more than 20 feet before the wave broke over me.

A man, black and scarred from a fire so now a ghost of himself, struck at me as he passed. From behind, a woman, cradling a ruined arm, pushed me. I didn't have their momentum, hadn't seen what they'd seen, what had triggered their panic. I was treading water, doomed to drown.

A pack of wild children, a tribe drawn out of the alleys and shadows by the smell of opportunity, suddenly surrounded me. Hungry eyes appraising my clean clothes, my worth, the contents of my worker's bag as I ran and they chased. A cramp in my side came on so suddenly, I thought for a fraction of a scream that one had knifed me with a piece of glass or a rusty sliver of iron or steel. Meat for the Dark Markets, old clothes for the camps. My breath was glass knives. My eyes were tiny and wind-burned from the cool night. My feet smashed, broke with each clawing stride.

They were jaguars. They were leopards. They were animals born and bred on the streets. And I was the sick member of the herd that day. I went for the alley. Stupid. So stupid. I moved, like drying clay, so slow, and they were there, blocking me in to bring me down and slice my throat.

The alley's mouth was fast approaching. Onto the sidewalk, around the stump of a telephone pole, my heart hammered in my head. I rounded the corner hard, driving an elbow hard into the chest and head of the (girl? boy?) I cut off. Behind me I heard the spill, the scrambling on the hard asphalt, the tumble as the pack tripped and spilled. I'd bought seconds, but no more.

Then the boy who'd caught me was hit from behind. A sudden force—very loud—slapped him down. He was naked save for canvas work pants five sizes too big, torn and filthy, tied around his waist and ankles with colorful wire. In one breath the boy had been there, turning to impale me with his knife—a rusty triangle of iron—and then he wasn't; he became a tumbling pile of arms and legs.

I didn't know the sound, couldn't recognize it.

I tripped and collided with the hard street. I waited for the knives, the teeth, the nails. But...nothing. Turning quick, I saw the alley, saw the cool darkness of the deep city, the running and cries of the riot far behind. Tubal stood between the riot and me, the bodies of three wild children a jumble of meat and blood streaks on the asphalt. He was breathing hard, holding the pistol to his chest.

"This is horrible," he said, pushing something vaguely purple with his fork. It was the Winter of '12, six months later, and most of the city was cold and starving.

Carved out of old industrial, the ceiling was low, framed by useless lead and copper wire, painted with thousands of coats of thick black. The place smelled of being rushed. An underground meeting place, a secret cave in a starving and freezing world.

"Amazing what you can do with garbage and camp rations," I said, trying to be cheerful. A riot the day before had been bad. Very bad. I couldn't wear or look at the shirt I'd been wearing. It wasn't my blood, but it was still blood. From somewhere. Shots, screams. I had begged Tubal to leave the pistol at home, to not take it with us when we went for our share of rations. The pistol made me nervous. He was angry with me, said maybe having it could have saved someone. I was angry in return: It could have gotten him killed. Or me.

"You need news?" said Geraldine. She was rare, and that made her special. Somehow she had managed to live in the nearby wilds and survive. Survive, gain weight, and dye her rat's nest purple. Too damned lucky, too damned informed, too damned exuberant. But she'd been around for years, and no one around her had vanished. Not many could say that.

"Give us the news, Gerry," Tubal said, pushing his plate of horrible purple improvisation aside and taking a long pull from the rotgut we were sharing. The polished tin can flashed and dazzled, distracting me from Geraldine pulling up an ancient folding metal chair.

I was the one who held the money. Funny how couples fall into their duties, their stations. I handed her a five, all crisp and unblemished, straight from Masoqui.

"Number two. Written in his blood," she said in her practiced storyteller's tone, tracking back and forth between us to catch our attention. "A pip-squeak manager down at the docks, but brother and son to the uppers. Dad's the District Superintendent, bro's the Militia Chief. Liked 'em young, street said. Chickenhawk. Made visits to the camps with his bro. Two go in, half a dozen leave. Liked his German rubber and his special machines a lot. Got good enough, streets say, to make some of 'em last the night. Good, but not good enough. Goes to the camp once a week. Once a week and six get the good life for a while, until the next itch comes."

Tubal pushed his tin can over to her. She took a quick swallow, put it back down, and smiled at him. "Was all lined up to take over. Seems bro was on the way up to New Jerusalem and they was goin' to make him Deputy Militia, maybe City Superintendent.

"Took him a while to die. Gagged, cuffed, and hung up high. Slit his ankles, deep enough to drain. Hung there all night, most of the day. Drip, drip, drip. Servants knew to not interrupt his pleasures, to let him alone. Didn't interrupt this, either."

I gave her another crisp five. Good news was rare, worthy of reward. "Bless Bourbaki," she said, giving the smile now to me, showing cracked and yellowed picket-fence teeth.

"God bless," I returned.

Tubal took his cup back, finished the rotgut, said, "I wonder how high it'll go."

Tubal didn't seem rough. It didn't seem to be in him; he was more polished, buffed, restrained. Seeing him, you'd think he'd be a cool, steel sword in bed, gleaming and strong.

And he was some of the time. But other times he wasn't what you might expect, and certainly not what I'd expected.

At first he was that sword, and his hands were strong and immaculate on my body: grabbing my ass in a tense grip, hand locked firm around my cock, mouth up and down on my dick like a well-balanced machine.

He seemed to pose in bed. Not prance, and certainly not preen. Pose, like a statue, like a carved marble edifice, cool and strong. I remember...was it the first time, the second? Hard to say. The date is gone, but even now the night burns in my memory. I'd been sucking him, teasing his long, muscular cock with the back of my throat. With a muscled arm like a piece of well-maintained machinery he scooped me up, hauled me to my feet like I was a cheap trinket. For a moment our cocks battled between us, hard-ons smacking together as we kissed.

Then he lifted me—a doll, a plaything—breathed steamy breaths on my chest. Then down, forcefully parting my thighs with a pair of quick, bruising slaps to my legs. I swallowed his throbbing cock with my ass. Drank him. The whole time, every moment of our fuck, his face remained frozen, immobile in control and determination.

He was like that most of the time. Not always—sometimes he got rough. I liked that too of course. For a long time.

Number Three: The Militia scurried into their holes and pulled the lids tight.

The newsletters, cranked out on some blotchy ink-jet system, flapped loose and free down the quiet street. Looking down from our second-story apartment window, I saw someone actually handing them out. Plain as day, bold as the brave. A smiling Aryan with a bone in his nose dressed in a new-looking Militia jumpsuit. *Cojones.* You could feel the Militia's hot eyes on him like a panicked tension in the air. He may have been found dead, later, but standing on Castro and Market, then, he was alive.

Our little birdie says that he won't be playing ball for a while, and in fact might be off the team. Hard to return a vicious volley when you have a handicap like that. No hands. No feet. We offer our sincere persecuted and murdered condolences to the Power and Water District Manager, and for the young victims of his reign, whose bodies are still being found in the Hunter's Point Wastes— and we applaud Bourbaki.

It was a Saturday. I know it was a Saturday because I wasn't at work, and Tubal would go out on long afternoon walks on Sundays. I remember my hands hurt from work, from twisting leads and jamming stubborn cables together. I had dozens of tiny cuts. I remember that we hadn't had sex for several nights because of my hands, or maybe because of the periodic chatter of gunfire that echoed down the streets from Civic Center.

"I wish they'd do something," I'd said, staring out the window. The city was hot, blasted by light, wavering in heat. The man with the fliers had wandered off.

"Who are you talking about?"

I can't remember what he was wearing or doing. I just remember the words, and the baking cement outside.

"I don't know—the Militia, Bourbaki. I don't know. I wish Bourbaki would cut all their damned balls off, castrate them, make them fucking all go away. I wish the Militia would kill him—kill us all."

"Just wish something would happen?"

"I just hate waiting, trying to expect everything. I'm tired of being surprised, is all."

"I don't know. Sometimes surprises can be good things."

"These days? Come on, we get a little, they take it back—and then some. Kill them or kill us. I'm just so tired."

"It's the heat. It can only get better."

"I wish it would just get...*something*."

"It'll get better." He touched me then, on my shoulder. I glanced back at him. He seemed so collected: not hot, not bored, not frightened. I remember looking away, suddenly angry with his smile, his constant relaxation.

"It'll get better."

"I just hate waiting. It reminds me of hospitals. Waiting rooms. Like when my father had his heart attack. Waiting to see if he was alive or dead. Now *we're* waiting to see if we're going to live or die."

Sometime that afternoon he told me. His family had a tiny bit of land near the Oregon border. He'd kept the place going, kept his father going, after his mother was raped and killed. The half-mad Militia had cut off her hands, cut off her breasts, and left her to die in the pigpen. He told me quietly, calmly, one word pushed slowly out of his mouth by another, how his father had changed after seeing his wife's blood mixed with pig shit, of the midnight visits paid to his 12-year-old son.

One winter he'd left. Not angry, not frightened. He just started walking. He left his father to die in the cold or from his own hand. He hitched a ride with a grain caravan, made his way to the city, to me.

"Things will always get better," he said. And even though there was something secret, something with blood in it, that he wasn't telling me, I believed him.

When he was rough...

On summer nights I'd dread the growl, for it meant having to wear long sleeves the next day. In winter the marks didn't matter so much; what warm clothes I had covered a multitude of sins. But winter had a cold edge to it, and a shortage of power and heating oil meant that every slap, bite, or punch hurt ten times worse.

Well, maybe not always, and sometimes it was a spice. Then other times when we kissed, when his hands went to my cock,and mine to his, when his lips touched my cock or mine touched his, the fear went beyond excitement, beyond adding blood to my dick. I'd shake, the fear rising in me. I'd shiver. In the winter sometimes he'd...sometimes stop, thinking I was too cold. Sometimes.

Other times his growl would build, swelling inside him as if tied directly to his throbbing dick. That growl signaled his ferocity. A kiss became a bite, the copper taste of my blood stoking his furnace. He'd grip me so hard I would groan more from the crushing of his hands than the thought of his bobbing dick.

The first blow would come, quick as lightning, with a practiced accuracy that would bend me over. Gagging, vomit surging up my throat, I'd bend—forced by pain rather than want. His cock would enter my throat with a lip-rending thrust, mixing his salty precome with acidic bile.

Or my asshole would take him, forced if it didn't open with enough speed; opening, then swelling in a great rectal swallow. I became a tube for him, a fuck hole for his thick cock. Lubricated with slime, spit, or blood; he didn't care.

I didn't know what to call it. It always made me hard. Even though it was rough, fast, and painful, and sometimes I didn't want it, I was always hard.

It wasn't until much later that I actually became afraid.

Another day—a Sunday (because Tubal wasn't there) in that summer of more vanishings, more numbered murders—someone called for him.

It was a rare occasion. I knew Tubal made calls, because sometimes he'd leave, right after dinner, right after sex, and go out "to make a call." I imagined him, standing in the dark, in the rain, making whispered arrangements to agents and provocateurs. He would go out even though we had a telephone, a ridiculous luxury Mr. Masoqui had managed to acquire for me. Phones were pretty rare, and making and receiving calls even rarer. A voice out of the air was unique. All I ever used it for was to call Citicore to check the system.

On this day it rang. "Is Peters there?"

"Don't know him. Have you got the right number?" The voice was nondescript, but not official. It lacked the practiced English and slapping timbre of Militia.

He recited it back. It was our number. "Tan, bald, mustache?"

"I don't know who you are. I don't know your voice."

"It's OK. Just tell him it's planted. Got that? It's real important. It's planted."

"I don't know what you're talking about."

"That's OK, just tell him. Planted, right? It's planted."

"I got the message, but I think you've got the wrong person."

"I don't think so. You just tell your pal."

"I'll tell him."

"Good. He enjoys his work. He'll enjoy this."

"I don't know what you mean."

"He gets a kick out of this, doesn't he? Your pal? He'll really like this. Makes him hard as a rock. I know, man. I know him from way back."

"Look, there isn't any Peters."

I still don't know what he was saying, telling me: a warning or a gloat. "He's always been like this. Been doing it since he was 9. Just worked his way up to bigger critters. More style, more flair. The man does love his work. Like his first one, stayed hard for weeks after. Couldn't wait to do number two. What's he up to now, anyway? Seven? Eight? More power to him. Man's found his niche."

I hung up on him.

Then it was winter. Time and our hero, Bourbaki, had given us names. Before, there was just *a place* where people might meet. In those days names could be used against us, so they weren't used. Now we could go to a little café called The Quiet Man, a little place with steamed windows.

It was days after the call, days to think and let it simmer. Dreams of guns, dreams of smiles, and the sound of shots. That morning in that street-side café: condensation running down glass, *me* telling *him* about it.

Numbers four and five had bought us room and time. Six had shoved the Militia down deep into themselves, into their fortified complexes high on the hills. Now they only came down to kill in the Tenderloin, in a firecracker pistol assault on the only area left to them. Stories circulated about foaming Militia shooting in impotent fury at old, already bullet-riddled buildings.

I told him of number seven and all he said was, "I wonder how high it'll go."

He vanished after that night in the café. I had looked at him and seen something I wasn't supposed to see.

So now I sit, drinking bootleg that is almost drinkable. Things have gotten that good. I sit in a café run and frequented by copies of myself. The Militia knows we are here, but won't risk the mutilations, the deaths, that Bourbaki would visit on them for one shot, one flaming bomb. Life is that good.

It's been two years since stumbling out of that ruin with yards of cable. Tubal was first a companion, then a hero. Now? Now I sit in The Quiet Man.

I have numbers to call, if I want. I could pick up one of the public phones, punch in a number and inform. Everyone knows Bourbaki, named after some mathematicians who tried to solve every paradox with numbers, with counting. They took the name of a French general, and failed.

I knew what *our* Bourbaki looks like, talks like—the man trying to solve our problems with his own numbers. I know what he smells like, the sounds he makes, his deep-down laugh, and who he might even love.

I might get shot for it, in revenge or as a reward. I might get a medal. Things might go back to the way they were. Things might go back to the fear of the gun, to bodies burning on the beaches, to friends vanishing like short dreams on waking, before a madman started killing all the right people.

I sit in The Quiet Man while people speak with laugher and joy about the doings of their hero. I sit with potato booze and try to decide to inform and betray, and maybe live. Or stay quiet and let him kill his secret with me.

As I sit here, I wonder: Am I still alive because he loved me, loves me? Or because I'm not worth counting.